BURN UNIT

T. Michelle

ISBN: 979-8-9864516-0-2

DEDICATION

To Sherrilynn, for pushing me outside of my comfort zone more than I could ever imagine, and constantly reminding me that I have a voice. Your passion is contagious, and I feel incredibly blessed to be able to learn from you always.
You've changed my life more than I could ever explain.
I love you.

To Grandpa, who I know would be bragging to anyone and everyone he passed by (stranger or not) that his granddaughter became a published writer.
Thank you for being such a huge part of my life.
I miss you.

PROLOGUE

The intense burning sensation escalating through my entire body was unbearable. As the scars started to form, I realized for the first time that this process was potentially going to kill me. I tried to breathe, but my lungs screamed with each agonizing blow. Every muscle I moved scratched at the scarred layers of skin that were sticking to my sheets. My vision blurred, and all I could comprehend seeing were the bright lights above me. I missed the feeling of walking, playing with my nieces and nephew, or simply eating a bowl of cereal. I had been stuck in here for so long I couldn't remember what day it was, and it seemed like I had seen every episode of every game show three or four times. I wanted to get out of this bed so badly, but it felt like that was never going to happen.

"This is probably a stupid question, but what's your pain level after that, sweetie?" she asked.

As I struggled to lift my hands up, she watched my face turn tomato red and told me to stop and relax. A couple moments later, a flood of cool breeze overpowered the fire under my skin, and I fell asleep. Even though it had only been a couple of hours, I felt like that was the most comfortable I had been in my entire life. I looked out the window of my dark hospital room, awaiting the day I would finally be released from the burn unit, and be home with the people I love; but where were they? Why has it been so long since Mom came to visit?

THREE MONTHS EARLIER

LIZZIE

"Mom, what happens to someone when they get set on fire?" my little brother asked. They were learning about the Salem Witch Trials in school, and he was always the curious one of the family. Everything went silent. Only the sound of the cereal crunching between our teeth echoed through the kitchen as I saw my mom's reaction to Jesse's question. "Deer in the Headlights" was a vast understatement, but at least she froze long enough that Jesse forgot about the question when he saw our neighbor, Max, outside the window. I heard her sigh as Jesse ripped open the front door to greet his bestest friend in the entire world.

"Duuuuuude that backpack is sick!" I heard him shout. Max was showing him the newest superhero backpack he got for his birthday. They sat on the front steps together talking about the new present, who they would be if they were superheroes, and what was for lunch at school today. I asked Mom what just happened and where that question came from. I just heard some silverware slip out of her hands and fall into the sink. I smirked and giggled a little inside. I waved to Max's mom, Kris, through the window. It was her turn to watch the kiddos get on the bus this week.

"I have no idea. I'm hoping he forgets about that," she replied. Her eyes twinkled with a glimmer of hope that a grade school kid's short-term memory lasted as long as a goldfish. I watched the two boys chat away through the front window until the bus pulled up to the driveway. Jesse ran in and screamed "bye!" to us as he and Max ran to join the rest of their clan on the big yellow above ground submarine. Standing outside the front door waving, I watched through the windows as five rambunctious boys fought over who got the window seat on the way to school. Out peeked Jesse, waving back at my mom and me, as we stood there watching the bus slowly pull away from the driveway. I love that kid. I went and started packing my bag and threw a face of makeup on while Mom finished the dishes. It seemed to be a good day so far. Mom wasn't usually this emotionally invested.

"Yo! We're going to be late!" I heard Mom scream from the bottom of the stairs. The hair on the back of my neck stood up.

"Mom! Don't say yo!" I screamed back. I almost face planted down the stairs as I stumbled down while trying to glide my shoes on. We both opened the car doors with such she-hulk strength, we could have torn the car in half. Mom sped out of the driveway, drifting around in a near circle as she narrowly missed everyone's mailboxes.

"Tokyo Drift doesn't have anything on me," I heard her mumble to herself. I just smiled and let her have her confidence this time. As long as I didn't miss Calculus today, I didn't care how we got there. Well, I actually just hoped she wouldn't embarrass me in the process. Sometimes, she was kind of the cool mom, even though she would never hear me admit it. I watched out the window at the houses flying past us as my mom sped through the residential streets.

"Mom, maybe let's not completely drag race through these streets," I suggested. She started to worry me with how reckless and unpredictable the drive was going. I heard a "pffffft" from her direction as we approached the intersection. My seatbelt choked me as Mom slammed on her brakes, narrowly avoiding a couple of teenagers that were crossing the street, teenagers that were from my homeroom. I sank down into my seat until the seatbelt was choking me and threw my backpack in front of my face hoping that they didn't see it was me. We rode the rest of the way to school in awkward silence.

"You have a good day, honey," Mom said as she kissed my forehead. "Were you staying after school today? What time do you need me to pick you up?"

"I'm helping with Ms. Wesley's Jr. STEM class today, so probably be done about seven-ish?" I replied. Mom gave me a thumbs up as I exited the car and ran across the street. I was going to be on time, but I had to hurry. I jumped into homeroom right before the bell rang. Sitting in front of me were the girls my mom almost ran over.

"Hey Speedy Gonzalez. Your mom better cool it before she kills someone…like me," one of them snarled, flipping her perfectly straight and smooth blonde hair.

"I'm too young to die!" the other dramatically shouted. Everyone busted out laughing before Mr. Morely walked in.

"What's going on in here?" I heard him curiously ask. I was too embarrassed to look, so I covered my face and headed to an empty desk on the far side of the room. I hoped I had avoided the embarrassment, but apparently news had spread like wildfire in this school. In a place where everyone knew everybody, there was no way someone didn't know. I knew I wasn't going to live this down for a while. We heard Principal Ellis start the morning announcements over the intercom, so we stood for the Pledge of Allegiance.

After we all seated ourselves, Mr. Morely handed out the calculus tests. I had anxiously awaited this test for so long. I crossed my fingers so that I could get through it smoothly. This was the last test before we found out if we did well enough to take the last trimester class for college credit. I looked at the first page and my eyes went cross-eyed, as the last three weeks of studying fluttered out of my brain and through that open window across the room.

"Good luck, students," Mr. Morely mentioned as he sat at his desk and pulled up to his computer. "I bet he's watching craft videos… or maybe he's streaming fail videos on there," my racing brain started to think. I shook the thoughts out of my head vigorously as I heard the clock ticking. It seemed like eight imprisoning years, but I got through the test. I prayed to whatever god that existed to give me a little sympathy. If I was going to fail, at least let me be right beneath that threshold so I could feel like I didn't completely blow it.

LIZZIE

A couple weeks ago, I was told to attend a school board meeting for my AP Government class. As I desperately attempted not to nod off in incessant, unspeakable boredom, I caught a moment in the meeting when they talked about concerns over the state of the crumbling elementary school, which piqued some interest amongst the crowded room.

"A recent assessment of the elementary school has found issues with the electrical system that require extensive repair. Issues surrounding this repair do include school closure for up to two weeks, possibly longer if asbestos is found," announced Mr. Davidson, superintendent for the school district. Even as a high school junior, my observations of Mr. Davidson weren't great. He wasn't known for putting his best foot forward and getting things done, meaning this so-called assessment was definitely not his call.

"And when will these repairs be done? With this timetable, we will need to plan on continuing the year through the summer. We would also need additional time to move around the budget, since this will be a significant development," a school board member spoke.

"Due to the impacts this project will have, I have already spoken to potential donors that will put up the money for the improvements, but they will have to wait until summer. This schedule also keeps us on track for keeping the budget as it is," Mr. Davidson answered. I felt my eyebrows furl a little bit in confusion; I found this odd. "School improvements don't come from private donors, usually. Right? What is he doing?" I watched one of the parents a few rows back stand up to speak.

"Excuse me. Putting politics aside, has anyone put to mind the safety for our children? If the electrical problems at the school are so immense, does that make it not safe for our kids? It's been known for years that improvements are desperately needed to be made for the school. YEARS! How much longer are you going to wait? Does something tragic need to happen to our children before you stand up and act?" she asked in an irritated tone. She clearly wasn't happy.

"Community members, I assure you I am taking student and teacher safety extremely seriously in the decisions made for this school. There are many factors to consider when making a decision of this caliber. I am aware that construction of the school is decaying, but I guarantee you, there is no reason to worry. School will resume as normal until summer vacation, and then the building shall shut down for the repairs," Mr. Davidson tried to ensure. I was just a kid, but even I didn't have a good feeling about this.

LIZZIE

Hours later after school ended, I walked myself down the road to the elementary school to help with Jr. STEM class. I came up to the familiar doors, hearing giddy, innocent laughter from inside. I peeked inside the gym to discover they are playing dodgeball today. Too bad they didn't have the giant parachute that I played with in my days. They were missing out hardcore. I met Ms. Wesley at her classroom door.

"Thank you soooooo much for coming. The project today is overwhelming me. Can you help me walk around and make sure everyone is understanding how to build these rockets?" she asked. She said it so fast, I had to take a second to register what she said.

"Oh, heck ya. I got this Wes. Don't worry about it," I assured her. Some days, I wondered why she, of all people, took over the STEM class for this group. Overwhelmed seemed to be her norm. I dropped my backpack on the ground and started walking around the tables, viewing everyone's projects. I grabbed one of the instruction sheets to skim through so I knew what they are supposed to look like, and then I jumped in on a couple tables to explain the concepts again; there were some tables where I had to show them where to connect the pieces. Everyone seemed to be having a good time though, so that was cool. The next minutes went by quickly, as there was always something to take care of and tables to assist.

We heard the fire alarm start screaming, which blasted us back into reality. Ms. Wesley and I gathered the group in a straight line and guided them out the doors to the front of the school. It wasn't the normal time to test the fire alarm, so a lot of the teachers were confused and a little bit worried. The alarm never went off, either, which was also strange. I heard another teacher behind me whisper under his breath that he thought the fire alarms were broken.

"Where is Mr. Davidson? What is going on?" Ms. Wesley leaned over and whispered in my ear her voice sounding shakier than usual. I shrugged my shoulders and shook my head. "I'm equally as clueless as you are, girl," I thought. After what seemed like 10 minutes, I started seeing what looked like smoke start billowing out of the roof from the back of the school. I turned to see teachers' faces start to go white. I remembered in the last school board meeting, someone mentioned that the elementary school needed electrical work done.

"Was that foreshadowing?" Mr. Davidson came hustling out and called the teachers over to him. I was conveniently standing close by, so I also unintentionally overheard the conversation.

"Teachers, first off, thank goodness most of the students have gone home, but we need to remain calm so the remaining students don't worry. There was a short in the cafeteria that set the ceiling on fire, which has now expanded to the overflow storage room. The fire department is on its way, and I've sent a mass text to the parents to come pick up their children if they can. We need to keep them away from the building as far as possible. No going to get homework, backpacks, or belongings. The school is now on lockdown," he announced. He wiped the sweat off his forehead and walked away from the group as the teachers stood there in shock and silence. I tapped on Ms. Wesley's shoulders and ushered her to the kids.

"We need to get everyone to the sidewalk," I whispered. She was still in shock from what she just learned. She started walking the students away from the building, and I walked over to the other teachers and ushered them to do the same with their after-school groups. Slowly but steadily, all the teachers started gathering their emotions and guiding their students to the sidewalk next to the street. I could hear sirens vaguely in the background. Without warning, we heard a loud explosion from behind us. My legs wobbled a little as they felt the ground shake. I turned around quickly to see the front of the school now engulfed in flames, and the power pole next to it was leaning heavily due to the blow. Teachers nearby started rushing their students away from the power line's path, until a loud crackling sound echoed through the air. The power pole, now on fire, dismantled from its base and was falling to the ground, endangering everyone around it. I watched as the pole seems to fall in slow motion, until I noticed that a couple of students that would not get out of the way in time.

Without thinking, I charged to the base of the pole and pushed the students out of the way as it plummeted to the ground. The weight of the pole landing on me felt as if it cut my body in half like a fancy magic trick, as the live power lines and hot flames laid across my body. My heart palpitated as potentially hundreds of thousands of watts of electricity pulsated through my body and the flames singed my skin. All I heard are cursing screams and loud sirens as 6,000 knives entered my body until I lost consciousness. "Shut off the power, now!" I heard in the distance. I woke later to sounds of the heart monitor reporting my heartbeat. My eyes could barely open from the burns, but I could feel the intubation tubes in my throat helping me breathe.

"Where am I? What happened? Is everyone okay?" I thought as I continued to come to consciousness, the pain of what just happened sat in. My heart started to race as my brain reported the pain to my receptors, and the memory of narrowly being burned alive flooded my mind. My muscles clenched and the monitor started screaming as my heartbeat neared dangerous levels, and I heard the sounds of doctors and nurses rushing in to help.

"Just relax. We are getting ready to take you to the hospital. You have burns and injuries that are the reason for the pain. We are giving you medicine to help. Try not to move, and relax," I heard vaguely as I passed back into unconsciousness.

I faded in and out of consciousness as I felt my body seemingly being thrown around like a ragdoll. In the distance, I could hear children crying and men talking about something over their walkie-talkies. I really didn't know what was going on. My thoughts continued to race in circles. "What happened? Did I jump in front of those kids? Wait, did something fall on me? Wait, why can't I feel anything beneath my waist? Where's Ms. Wesley? Where's Mom?" I continued to fade in and out from the shock of the searing pain that was enveloping me. I felt mists of water fill the air as firefighters continued putting out the flames and started investigating the damage.

"What's the extent of the damage?" someone spoke over the walkies.

"What I can see right now is that the explosion caused massive structural damage through the central corridor. Lunchroom and storage area completely destroyed. Chance of collapse high," replied the other side. "Power will not be restored to the premises until further investigation is completed. Keep everyone out of the building."

I couldn't move. I could barely breathe. Every muscle contraction reminded me that layers of flesh just burned away from my body. Pieces of my scorched, blistered skin started to peel away, seemingly giving up from the trauma it just endured. I felt myself being rolled onto a stretcher, scratching the layers of skin still trying to stay on. I felt unbearable pain in my lower back. It felt like something ripped my spine in half. My thoughts continued to spiral. I could only remember glimpses and flashes, but I was still confused and couldn't remember what exactly happened? "What was it? What did I do? I only remember ushering kids to the sidewalk. I keep seeing flashes of sparks and hearing sticks break. What happened? I didn't go into the building, did I? Did I? Why do I smell things burning? Why can't I feel my legs?"

I tried desperately to remember anything

from the last 24 hours. Anything. I could only open my eyes far enough to notice I was moving, although not of my own accord.

"H-h-hhh-hhhey," I managed to muster. The EMT on my side looked at me in horror, realizing that I somehow survived something I still couldn't remember.

"Hey there. Uhmmm, I need you to stay calm…. Aaaaaand don't move," he replied. His voice startled me. Why did he sound so panicked and worried? It was like this was his first time on a call.

"W-w-w-wwwhat?" I mustered out before I started coughing up dark clumps of dirt mixed with blood. I felt the stretcher stop moving as eight hands gently pressed my body back to a lying position. A towel patted my face to wipe away the mess, and a second EMT told me to lie down and try not to move.

"You were in an accident, and you are really injured. We really need you to remain calm. We are going to do our best to take care of you," I heard faintly as I lost consciousness. The next time, I didn't wake up as easily. Instead, I saw what looked like fireworks in my dreams.

I dreamt of the fireworks celebration at the Harvest Festival last fall with my great grandmother. That was her last show before we had to put her in a nursing home. We couldn't take care of her anymore due to Mom's schedule, and her dementia had gotten worse. I thought to myself, "I wonder if she remembers me. Last time I visited her, she knew who I was, but forgot whose family I was from. Wait. How bad was this accident? I still don't remember an accident. Wait, what accident? Where is everyone?"

Before I knew it, I woke up to the sounds of stretcher wheels squeaking through a cold hospital hallway, and a heart monitor screaming at nearby nurses. I still couldn't move my body without feeling the wrath of Hades wash over my skin, that is, when I could move. I managed to barely lift my hand into my peripheral vision and saw the charred remains of what used to be my skin clinging to my bones. "Holy shit, what happened?" My arm started to shake as panic set into my brain. I attempted to scream, but sound didn't escape, and I couldn't breathe. The heart monitor started screaming louder, and I heard nurses yelling "no no no no no" and trying to keep my arms down without touching me.

"Nurse, Let's get a Propofol drip going so this patient isn't using unnecessary muscle function. We need to get her into a medical coma right away. Do you hear me? Let's get two mg of Morphine into her IV for pain management," I heard a stern voice command. "Lizzie, can you see me? Can you hear me?" he asked. I twisted my head and opened my eyes just enough to see a tall man with a white coat hovering over me. "You were in a severe accident that left a lot of your body burned. We cannot have you moving too much, or your skin can tear, and there is a possibility your heart can stop. I need you to do something for me. I need you to…" His voice drifted away as I felt a cool breeze come over my body from the morphine, and I drifted off to sleep. I never heard what he needed me to do.

The next time I woke up, I lifted my eyelids just enough to see what looked like a dark hospital room. The heart monitor continued to beat at every heart movement, and I was already wanting to throw it out the window. I felt tightness around my entire body. Doctors and nurses had painstakingly wrapped my entire body in bandages to hold my delicate skin in place. I didn't have the energy to wonder where I was anymore. After hacking my lungs out and coughing out more blood, the nurse rushed in to give me more morphine, and I drifted off to sleep.

Messy...Memories

LIZZIE

Jesse and I loaded our belongings into the car while Mom and Dad fought in the driveway again. This was the first weekend in months that Dad offered to let us stay with him. As it always does, his job called him in again, so he called Mom and asked her to come get us. She yelled about the obscene drive it took to get there and how she had to take time out of her life for this. Jesse asked if everything was okay, to which I answered "yes" and distracted him with his videogames. Something didn't feel right about Mom saying she had to take time out of her life, but I brushed it aside because I knew she didn't really know how to communicate when she was that emotional. At least that explanation made sense to me.

"Look, I'm sorry, okay? If I miss this, then I lose my job and the ability to pay your sickening request for child support. You really want that?" he blurted out. Mom folded her arms and pouted at the thought, then tried to fight with Dad about something else she didn't like. Dad cut off the conversation, walking back into his house and shutting the door without listening to Mom's persistent yelling. She gave up and marched back to the car, practically growling as she set the car to drive and swung out of the driveway. Jesse opened his mouth to ask what was wrong before I placed my hand over it and shook my head quickly. "Just focus on your videogames kid. This is not a conversation we need to escalate." I could've thought I could see smoke coming out of her ears at one point.

Sophie met us at the house and helped unload the trunk. Mom vented to her about the whole situation and how she was then late for the Newscasters' Ball the station was having, I guess. Sophie stayed quiet and just took the brunt of Mom's anger. She offered to stay with us while Mom went to the party and ushered her out the door as quickly as she could to get the yelling out of the house. After we sat in the quiet for a while, Jesse asked if Mom was okay and why she was mad. Sophie stumbled over her words trying to explain what was going on without unloading the family drama onto such a young kid.

"Jesse, nothing is wrong. Mom is just having a hard day. She wasn't feeling good. Nothing is your fault, okay? Neither one of you. This is between Mom and Dad." I nodded and leaned into Sophie, who put her arms around both of us. We sat in each other's arms with the sound of the television in the background lulling everyone to sleep.

LIZZIE

I walked back to the car with the test results in hand from the AP English test I had taken the previous week. I swung the papers in the air for Mom to see. After shutting the car door, I announced that I passed the test, adding to the college credits I was earning before I graduate. Mom clapped for joy and honked the horn too many times while screaming out the window that her baby was a genius. I felt the redness warm up my face, and my legs started to get wobbly. As we drove out of the parking lot, I asked if we could go to the nursing home to show Grandma Faulkner. Maybe this could be a good reason to make the drive that she always hated. Mom sat in thought for a moment and groaned a little bit, perhaps because I was right. She agreed to the trip, but she mentioned that we had to pick up Jesse first. She also told me I had to help with dinner that night in return.

I agreed while I rolled my eyes, and we made the long, boring trip to the nursing home.

Jesse charged across the parking lot to grab the front door of the home, only for it to magically open by itself. He turned back to us amazed at the enchanting power he had to make doors open. Mom told him to wait and to hold her hand while they walked through the building. The hallways were bare and a little haunting at times. The cold, white walls and echoing sound of canes on the tile floors left little to be desired. Most residents were in their rooms still, with a small few playing pinochle in the great room. We signed in at the visitors' desk and walked down the next hallway to Grandma's room. She was sitting in front of her window watching the birds singing in the pear tree planted just on the other side of the glass. She turned to see us, and her smile stretched farther than the width of her face. She embraced us with the familiar warmth we were so used to, hugging us and never wanting to let go.

Jesse began telling her endless stories of playing with his friends and the newest toys he was putting on his birthday list. Grandma almost had to cut him off to ask me how school was going. I showed her the test results I received earlier that afternoon. She gave me a great big hug and bragged to her nurse about how proud she was of us great grandkids. She even mentioned our older sister,

Sophie, and how she got married and had three kids, and how great of a mom she was.

"Leslie, aren't you so proud of these kids?" she asked, looking over at Mom. Mom nodded her head with a smirk on her face and rolled her eyes a little bit. Her eyes quickly settled back at her phone.

"They are good kids, aren't they?" she replied. She quietly stood in the background as all Grandma's attention turned to us kids once more, encouraging us and telling us how much she loved us. She asked if we were hungry; she mentioned that she had made dinner that day and wanted to make sure we had something to eat. We looked at her in confusion "Was this another dementia slip?" Jesse nodded his head in excitement for the treats that were being offered; Neither of them realized we were in a nursing home, and Grandma didn't cook anymore. Grandma's nurse hustled out of the room to find something to offer my rambunctious brother, coming back with a couple cookies and a cup of pudding. That was enough for Jesse to calm down and sit on the bed as he swallowed his treats whole. We were there for another couple of hours, catching up and hearing stories from Grandma's life. She was so proud of us.

The next day, Mom planned a family dinner and invited Sophie and her husband, Chris, to the house. My nieces and nephew were running around the house chasing Jesse playing cops and robbers while I sat on the couch studying for the next big test. I could overhear the adults at the kitchen table talking about life and how hard it had been juggling careers and kids, Sophie empathizing with Mom about also juggling a rough divorce in the middle of it. Mom took all the sympathy she could get. She always talked about how hard it was feeling like she had to do it all alone, and how Dad seemingly never supported her, even when they were married. As Sophie tried to change the tone of the conversation, Mom continued to go on about Dad's flaws.

"Leslie, maybe not go so hard on the father of your children…. In front of your children," Chris bravely mentioned, clearing his throat. The comment prompted a moment of silence before Mom rolled her eyes and turned to grab food to put on the table. Sophie sighed and mouthed "thank you" to her husband while squeezing his hand before getting up and helping move food around and rounding up the younger kids. Everyone sat for an awkwardly silent dinner before Jesse started telling the new jokes he learned at school. They went over huge with Sophie's kids, but jokes about sweaty socks went right over the grown-ups' heads.

MARK

Mark and Holly walked into the swanky, new Italian restaurant and announced their reservation name with the waiter standing at the door. They were ushered to a small table in the corner, lit up with dim ceiling lamps and candles at the table. Holly looked around at the vintage décor, admiring the wood detailing around the walls, and the hand painted portraits hanging on the walls. Mark didn't have the same love for detail that Holly had, but he continued to nod his head every time she asked if he had seen the next new feature she had discovered. He smiled, watching his girlfriend turn into a little kid, distracted by all the new sounds and sights of the restaurant they had talked of going to for weeks since it had opened.

"Mark, this place is amazing! Thank goodness you were able to get the night off, finally!" she exclaimed. The waiter came and introduced himself, talked about the menu set up, and filled their waters. After ordering their favorite wine and the charcuterie board to appetize on, Holly continued to chat about her day while Mark sat by half-listening. Realizing he was clearly uninterested in the conversation, she asked him about the kids and how his time was with them earlier that week.

"Work got me out of it. They were at my house for just four hours before I had to have Leslie pick them up. Granted, the trip to get them is long as hell, so they were here for about the length of a workday, but that woman is toxic. Those kids don't stand a chance," he explained. Holly asked why he didn't do anything more, only to be followed by Mark explaining how his career didn't give a lot of room for children. She suggested that anything could give the room for children, if he made room, to which Mark rolled his eyes and downed the rest of his wine. Mark changed the subject to the new promotion and how much he had to take on in addition to his responsibilities before, and Holly listened intently to how he was getting along with the new gig. He continued to update her on the workplace drama as their main courses of carbonara and alfredo arrived at the table.

"This food is incredible!" Holly continued to exclaim with every new bite she took. Mark let out a geeky, little smirk every time Holly spoke up. He soaked up the childlike joy she showed being in this new restaurant.

"Plus, if we had kids, we wouldn't be able to go to these places all the time," he commented. Holly rolled her eyes while she ate, eyeing the family in the booth across the restaurant from them. They continued with their night, conversing about their days and where they wanted to go next. Mark mentioned he had a surprise for Holly. They cleared their plates, and Mark paid the bill. They gathered their leftovers in their to-go bags and walked through the doors of the restaurant. Mark ushered Holly around the corner to the park that was nearby. They followed the walking path through the groves of trees and past the occasional family picnicking on the grounds.

They came to a fountain that laid hidden within the park. Mark took another gulp of his to-go wine and told Holly that his boss had told him about the fountain. Holly basked in the natural beauty that surrounded the water feature, and she dug through her purse looking for any kind of coin she could find. Mark dug a quarter out of his jacket pocket and laid it in her hand. She turned her back to the fountain, put her head down for a moment, and then she tossed the coin over her shoulder and into the shallow water. They continued the walking path until they returned to the parking garage.

SOPHIE

Sophie hurried through the house trying to find her keys that were hidden by her children when they were playing games the previous night. One child was running around the house flying invisible airplanes, while another struggled to put their shoes on the right feet. Her husband, Chris, dragged their oldest child out of the bathroom wrapped in towels. He discovered the young one was throwing every bath toy into the toilet and trying to see if they could disappear, to no avail. Chris admitted to Sophie that the bathroom was a disaster, but they would clean it later. He encouraged her to continue getting ready to go and to not worry about the disaster that awaited them. After what felt like a hurricane of preparation, they set off on the road trip to visit the family.

Sophie's heart melted when she watched her children play with her younger brother, who was around the same age. She smiled at all the jokes only they understood and the closeness that always returned even after weeks of not seeing each other. As the little ones ran around the house playing every imaginary game they could, she soaked up the moments she was able to spend time with her younger sister. Having graduated college not too long before she started her family, she saw a lot of herself in Lizzie. Lizzie wanted to be a veterinarian or a doctor, and Sophie always tried to remind her little sister of what would be required. Little did she know that Lizzie would soon double the amount of AP classes she herself had taken, and Lizzie held all her comments as a challenge that she would prove in the future.

Sophie sat at the table quietly listening to her mother complain about her father's faults, wanting to say something but not knowing how to stand up to the most powerful force in her eyes.

Luckily, Chris cleared his throat and spoke up, relieving some of her fears. It worked for a time, but the strain between Sophie and her mother had already become apparent since the divorce. Sophie had already moved out when her parents split, but she noticed something change in her mother that wasn't pleasing in her eyes. It made her worry about her younger siblings, whether they would be able to handle how unpredictable their mother's personality had become. Late at night, she rambled on her concerns to Chris, who always laid in bed quietly listening until Sophie fell asleep.

THE TRUTH

LESLIE

"Five minutes until roll call!" Leslie heard from her office. It was a busy news day, so she was excited for what stories she was reporting on next. A small drug bust on the edge of town, tractor parade for Planting Week, and a city grant given for wastewater management were highlights of the day. She cleaned up her makeup, slid her stilettos back on, and strutted out the door to the anchor seat. On her way out, she heard whispers from the production crew around her. The environment had a different feel at that moment, which was strange. She ignored the secrets, looks, and whispers and continued on, but not after a quick check to make sure she didn't have toilet paper sticking out of her skirt. She sat in her chair and adjusted her clothes to prepare for screen time. One of the producers came up to hand her the reports.

"I'm surprised you're still here," he mentioned.

"Why would I not be?" Leslie asked with a confused look.

"Well, here are the reports for this evening. Long story short, cattle drive scheduled tomorrow, so roads will be blocked; commissioner named for Planting Week celebration; and a fire at the elementary school. I'm sorry," he explained and hurried away.

"Roll on Two!" the director stated. Leslie was still trying to process the information when he said, "Action!"

"Welcome to our evening news, everybody!" Leslie proclaimed with a smile. "Breaking news tonight. A short in the electrical system at the elementary school caused a fire that destroyed much of the building. All elementary school students and teachers got out safely, reports Superintendent, Jack Davidson. The only casualty is a teen who heroically pushed in-danger students out of the way of a burning power pole which unfortunately fell on top of her. She is currently in critical condition at the community hospital." She paused. The pieces suddenly fell into place, and everyone's odd behavior finally made sense. "Excuse me, I will be turning the rest of the time to my co-anchor for tonight." She slid the copy to her co-anchor and walked off the set like a zombie. Shock set in as she realized why people were whispering and looking her way. Why the producer told her he was sorry. She kicked off her stilettos and picked them up off the ground as she started to run to her office to grab her keys.

"What are you doing?" the news station president asked.

"My daughter was the one who saved those kids. My daughter is the one in the hospital in critical condition. I have to go," she explained while fighting the cracks in her voice.

"You do realize you just left a set in the middle of taping, right? One of those cardinal rules?" he mentioned.

"You do realize my daughter may die today, right?" she barked back. Her heart was pounding. He shook his head in disapproval and walked away. Leslie grabbed her phone and called her neighbor, Kris. The answering machine picked up.

"Kris, I need your help. Will you please watch Jesse for a while? I just found out what happened at the elementary school, and I'm on my way to the hospital. Please, please call me back as soon as you can," she pleaded into the phone before hanging up. There weren't any texts from Lizzie.

Usually there was something talking about what was up in class today. Her hands became clammy, and they started to shake as she hurried to her car. She narrowly missed the dumpster as she backed out of the parking lot and raced to the hospital. "Why did no one call me? What happened? Where is everyone?" were the only thoughts racing through her head. The town was bustling with excitement preparing for Planting Week, which meant more traffic than the town has seen for a long time. Leslie desperately tried to hold it together as she repeatedly got stuck behind tractors, semi-trucks, and delivery drivers that were slowing her down. Tears started streaming down her face as the reality sat in about the situation. Her daughter could die. Her breathing escalated as she started thinking of what could have gone through her daughter's mind. "Why did she do that? What injuries does she have? Will she be okay? Why did she do that?!" she thought while slamming her hands on the steering wheel.

Her thoughts turned to how serious Lizzie's injuries could be. "A burning power pole fell on top of her. Surely the weight broke something. But it was burning. Did she have burns? Were the wires live? What happened to my baby girl?" Her mind broke, and she struggled to breathe. Panicked tears started welling up in her eyes. She narrowly missed a stalled tractor on the side of the road as her attention jumped back to driving. The 10 minutes to the hospital felt like five long, grueling hours. Leslie looked to the area of the elementary school and saw a faint shadow of smoke rising into the air. Her heart pounded at the thought of what she was to find when she got to the hospital.

Leslie slammed the door closed as she raced to the hospital doors. Her heart continued to pound as she prepared for potentially devastating news. Once inside the waiting room, she noticed there was no one there.

"Help! Please help!" she screamed, looking for someone that could give her some semblance of answers. A nurse charged out from the back room and asked what was wrong.

"My daughter was at that elementary school. Where is she?" Leslie asked.

"What's your daughter's name?" the nurse questioned.

"Lizzie. My daughter is Lizzie. Where is she?!" Leslie screamed.

"Miss., I need you to calm down, okay. I remember someone being checked in whose name was Lizzie. Let me see what I can find out, okay? Can you sit down for me?" the nurse struggled to utter. She had lied. She knew about Lizzie. The heartbreaking nightmare that got rolled in on an ambulance, her skin almost blackened. How could she tell the mother of this patient that it didn't look good? She raced down the hallway to find a doctor.

"It's too quiet in here. Why is there no one here? Why is no one rushing?" Leslie asked herself as she waited. From around the corner, she saw a man in a white coat covered in blood walking towards her. She raced to him.

"Where is she? Where is my daughter? I want to see my daughter!" She screamed in agony.

"Miss, I need you to calm down, okay? Let's sit down," the doctor tried to explain. Leslie refused.

"I… need… to see… my daughter!" she continued to scream.

"Miss, I really need you to calm down. We can't have this hysterical behavior in the waiting room," he requested in a louder, more commanding voice. Leslie wiped away her mascara, smearing tears all over her face and just dropped to the floor. The doctor kneeled to be face to face with Leslie.

"My name is Doctor James. Your daughter Lizzie was transported to this location in critical condition. We are still examining the extent of her injuries. Right now, we can confirm that she does have breaks in three vertebrae in her back, and she does have third degree burns over more than 45% of her body. Heart monitors are also showing some signs of potential electrocution in the accident. Again, we are still trying to examine just how severe her injuries are, but that is what we know right now. I must be completely honest, Miss. It doesn't look good for Lizzie. Even if she does manage to make it, it's going to be a long and excruciating road to recovery, and there's a potential she may never be able to walk again," he explained. Leslie broke down. It became more and more real that her daughter at that point was an atom of what she once was. Her chances were slim to none for survival.

"How do I tell my son? How do I tell her father? She was so close to graduating, and even graduating early. How much pain is she in? What are they doing to help her? This is going to kill her grandmother. Why didn't I say no to her helping today?" She continued to beat herself up for letting Lizzie help that day instead of having her stay home. "She should have stayed home and studied. She has applications to figure out for college. She shouldn't be here…." Leslie's mind hopped back into reality and turned to the doctor who was then walking away.

"Wait, doctor. Is there any way I will be able to see my daughter?" she asked desperately.

"At this time, she is still in the operating room. We are doing the best we can to help her and clean her up. I will keep in touch with you about any updates we come across," he replied. He put his hand on her shoulder briefly and continued to walk away. Leslie was left standing alone in the hospital waiting room, the faint sound of the intercom calls and monitors in the background. She found her way to an empty chair, sat down, and began to sob in her hands. She sat sobbing at the idea that life was going to be completely different.

Completely different for not only the family, but Lizzie herself. She had set plans on what she wanted to do with her life and was well on her way to accomplishing them. Leslie sat in disbelief, still trying to process everything she has witnessed in the past couple hours. She leaned over and picked her phone out of her purse. There were two missed calls and eight unread text messages. She paused for a moment to gather herself enough to make the calls to the family. As much as she didn't want to admit it, she needed their help.

MARK

"So, gentlemen, as you can see, first quarter profits are at quite high marks, may I add. If you open your debriefings to page six, you will see the itemized schedulings that are ready for approval in an attempt to take full advantage of our new budget for the second quarter," Mark explained as he paced the front of the fully seated meeting room. His promotion six months ago put a lot of grey in his hair, but that was his favorite part of the job. There was something about essentially saying "I told you so" to his much older co-workers and comrades that just put a fire in his belly. The meeting adjourned for the end of the day, and everyone packed up their shiny, black briefcases and started heading out, but not without shaking hands and congratulating the young lad who essentially doubled their money in a matter of months. Mark followed the others out of the meeting room, only to separate and head to his office to phone his girlfriend, Holly.

"Hey sweetie, how did your day go?" he asked softly.

"It went well. I went to the pharmacy and picked up my medication, met my mother for lunch at that place we found last week, and now I'm here at home gathering things together. How was the meeting? Any nay-sayers like last time?" she asked. As Mark explained how much of a success the meeting was, and what people were saying, he sensed something wrong in Holly's voice.

"Honey, something is up. What's going on?"

he asked curiously. He heard Holly clear her throat.

"Mark, sweetie. There was an accident at the elementary school where you used to live," she started to explain.

"Wow, didn't know that building would even stand this long," he broke in.

"Mark, listen. Even though all the children and teachers were okay, they're saying that there was one teen that stepped in to help some of the kids and…. They don't know if she will live," Holly explained hesitantly.

"So? My boy's in a school on the other side of town, and he's only eight. Why is this important?" Mark asked somewhat snarkily.

"Mark, it's Lizzie. A power pole fell and, she was under it. The injuries they are saying she has are horrifying. Maybe, you should call your ex-wife" she suggested. There was a long silence before Mark said anything more.

"Lizzie. My Lizzie? She doesn't go to that school. She's a teenager. You know that."

"Mark, she helps with after-school activities there. You know that," Holly mentioned, not meaning to repeat Mark as if she was mocking him. Her body cringed at the sound of the words that came out of her mouth.

"So. She wasn't there. They have the wrong kid. Did you verify this information?" Mark asked. "You know how Leslie can be."

"Mark, STOP! Listen to yourself. Your daughter was THERE! She was hurt. She's in critical care in the hospital, and they're saying she might not make it! I'm gathering things together so we can go down there. When will you be home? Will you pleeeaaase call your ex-wife?" Holly pleaded. Mark gave her a timeline of a few minutes and grumpily ended the call. "I don't know what she is talking about. That wasn't my daughter. Sometimes I wonder if she's as delusional as my ex," he thought to himself.

Mark rolled his eyes as he looked toward his cell phone on the corner of his desk. He turned it off earlier that day so he wouldn't be bothered as he prepared for the day's meeting. He grabbed the device, pressed the power button, and waited for it to turn on. After about 30 seconds of powering up, Mark just heard *Ding! Ding Ding! Ding! Ding!* as the phone notifications caught up. He wiped his hair back and looked down. Three missed calls and five unread texts from Leslie. He grumbled obscenities to himself before initiating a call back.

"Mark? Mark, are you there?" Leslie

frantically asked.

"Yes, Leslie. I'm here. How can I possibly help you?" Mark replied with a stern and sarcastic voice.

"Don't give me that. Your daughter was in an accident at the school and is in the hospital. We're talking burns, broken bones, paralysis, possible electrocution. They don't know if she's going to make it," she answered, speaking so quickly Mark could barely understand it.

"And you know it's Lizzie how? Don't tell me your little gossip writers told you about it," Mark snarled.

"Don't start this. You know that promotion of yours came with a lot more benefits than I have ever had. And no. I'm here at the fucking hospital, like a worried, panicked mother should be, and I'm talking to the doctor as much as I can. You wanna give me a fucking break?" Leslie yelled through the phone.

"Whatever. I guess Holly has already decided that we're coming to town. So, we'll figure out the truth then." Mark slammed the phone on his desk. The screen cracked from the force of the blow, and Mark tossed the phone into his briefcase and slammed the lid. He stomped out of the building and kicked his way to his Bentley. Heavy rock music blared through the radio as he started the ignition and drove to meet Holly at their apartment.

"I guess we're ready to go?" Mark asked as he walked into the front entrance only to see suitcases near the door.

"Just needed your human remains is all," Holly replied, trying to make light of the situation. She handed him suitcases and pushed him out the door. She locked up the house and met at the trunk of the car to help Mark load everything up. After about five minutes of trying to pack things into the trunk, they both hopped into the car, awaiting the long trek to Mark's hometown to find "the truth."

The trip to Mark's hometown was quiet, anxious, and mind-numbingly nauseating. Holly drove while Mark sat in the passenger seat, tapping his foot up and down nearly the whole way. Mark re-adjusted the seat every couple minutes, never able to find a comfortable position. Holly clacked her teeth to pass the time while she drove, the GPS screaming at them which turns to make. After what seemed like the entire afternoon, they arrived at the hospital and hurriedly charged into the emergency room. Leslie had beat them there and was pacing in her stilettos and designer bag. She walked up to the receptionist's desk over and over again asking where her daughter was.

Holly urged Mark to sit down while she figured out what was going on. She tapped Leslie on the shoulder and waved hello while Leslie continued to command the nurse to give her the information she was entitled to. Holly mouthed "I'm sorry" to the nurse, who was then showing deep concern. Leslie eventually walked away in frustration to sit down, leaving Holly to seemingly pick up the mess.

"I apologize. She can be a lot. Uhmmmm…. I'm Holly," she introduced, giving a hand to shake for the nurse. "I'm Lizzie's stepmom… kind of… her father's girlfriend. Wwhhh…. What's happened?"

"Hi, Holly. I'm Lyla," the nurse replied. Her voice shook as she tried to keep her composure from her altercation with Leslie. "Lizzie is currently being cleaned up. We still don't know the full extent of the damage, but she is alive… a… and… we will do our best to take care of her."

"Thank you, Lyla. Do you happen to know when we might be able to see her?" Holly asked.

"Probably in a few minutes. I'll find out when we are moving her to the ICU, and I can have you guys see her briefly in the hallway. You won't be able to touch her, but you can at least see her alive," Lyla encouraged. Holly nodded her head and sat herself in the chair next to Mark. She leaned over and relayed the information to Mark, and they patiently waited for Lyla to return to the desk. About 30 minutes later, Lyla stood from the desk and urged the parents to follow her. They walked down a couple of quiet, sterile hallways until Lyla stopped and put an arm out to usher them to do the same. The large, metal doors to the emergency room opened, nurses and doctors leading the bed and IV stands with them to move Lizzie.

As Lizzie's near lifeless body appeared in the hallway, Leslie provided a dramatic interpretation of a soap opera, yelling for her baby. A couple of doctors warned her that she needed to calm down or she would be removed, but she didn't listen. She was urged by a couple of the nurses back to the waiting room. Mark's face went pale. His daughter was still covered in grey ash, her face mangled from the accident. Dried blood stuck to her long, blonde hair. Most of her body was covered with gauze and strategically placed bandages. Whatever skin was visible appeared blackened by smoke and ash. Holly looked over and saw the terror in Mark's face, grabbing his arm and asking if he was okay. Mark turned to cover the tears in his eyes, and he walked himself back to the waiting room. He made it halfway before finding an extra chair on the way, sitting down and putting his head in his hands. Holly told Lyla "Thank you," shook her hand again, and gloomily walked over to Mark to be by his side.

WHAT NOW?

LESLIE

Leslie sat at her dining room table with her oldest daughter Sophie, and son-in-law Chris. After sending the young kids out to the yard to play, she struggled to figure out what to say to console her eldest children.

"It's been two weeks, but it feels like it has been years," she stated, wiping occasional tears from her face.

"I agree. I feel so helpless because I live farther away. It sucks to see Lizzie like this. You said Dad was staying in town for a bit?" Sophie asked.

"Ya. I guess he has a buddy a couple miles away who has extra room, so he's staying there. I'm just glad he believes me now," Leslie answered. Sophie shook her head and rolled her eyes when her mother wasn't looking.

"What's going to happen now?" Chris bumped in.

"Still unsure. Her back is broken in four places, and one of the vertebrae in her lower back pinched her spinal cord, so she may not be able to walk again. Luckily, the electrocution wasn't as bad as they originally thought, but almost 45% of her body has third degree burns, so they're talking about months of recovery. They have her in a medically induced coma so her body can focus on healing," Leslie explained. Chris leaned over to comfort his wife as Sophie started to sob. "The hard part is," Leslie continued, "is how hard Jesse has taken this. He's so worried all the time, and I've had two calls from his teachers that he hasn't been paying attention in class or turning in paperwork, and there's a chance he was a suspect in a fight that started at his school. It's scaring me just how much he's changing through this." Sophie squeezed her mother's hand in solace.

"We probably need to keep as much of this under wraps as we can, to protect him," she suggested.

A knock at the door interrupted the conversation. Mark and Holly arrived to take the kids to the park while Sophie, Chris, and Leslie headed to the hospital for updates.

"Are you sure you don't want to go, Mark?"

Holly asked.

"No," he answered firmly. After hearing from the doctor and seeing the sight of his child covered in ash, he had refused to walk back into the hospital since. The group parted ways, and the kids got belted in the car to go to the park. One kid needed to sit on Holly's lap, since the Bentley wasn't equipped for a large family. It was a quiet ride to the park, other than the youngest not enjoying the car seat. The music wasn't even playing on the radio. Holly tried to make small talk while in the car, asking the kids how school was and what they did earlier that day, but Jesse wouldn't talk at all. He simply stared out the window watching cars go by. Mark peered into the rearview window to see his young son hunching down into the seat.

"We're going to get through this, son," Mark tried to explain. Jesse sat in silence. Not hearing a response, Mark said it again. "Son?"

"How do you know?" Jesse barked back.

"Hey, don't start with me. We are all worried about Lizzie, okay? But the only thing we can do is hope the doctors can help her," Mark said sternly. "What is up with you lately? Not paying attention in school AND starting a fight?"

"I didn't start the fight."

"Jesse, tell me the truth," Mark repeated.

"I didn't start it! Plus that… what do you think? My sister is gonna die, and my parents don't care about me anymore," Jesse replied.

"Lizzie's not going to die! Where did you get that from?" Mark asked as he parked the car. Holly nodded toward Mark to say she would get the kids out of the car. He turned back to face Jesse.

"Ever since Lizzie got hurt, Mom keeps walking around the house saying Lizzie is going to die. Everyone ignores me. I'm a person too!" Jesse explained.

"Jesse, I'm sorry you've been hearing that over again. I promise you; Lizzie is not going to die. I'm sorry a lot of our attention has been on Lizzie lately. But do not let that convince you that I or your mother do not love you. You are equally a part of my life as Lizzie and Sophie are, okay? How are things going at home other than what your mom has been saying?" Mark asked.

"No one's there. Lizzie's not home. Mom's never home, and when she is, she's talking about Lizzie. Mom's been letting me go to Max's house after school. Kris likes to talk about Mom. She said Mom had too many kids since I always have to go to her house. She says that Mom shouldn't have had any kids," he revealed. Mark pursed his lips and paused to think.

"I will talk to Kris, but it sounds like something definitely needs to change," Mark started. "Something needs to change… What if I started to pick you up from school sometimes? The house I'm staying at isn't too far away. We can spend a little more time together, and I can show you that I'm not ignoring you." Everything stood still for a moment while the young Jesse thought. After a while, he smiled and nodded and then jumped out of the car to go join Holly and the other kids on the merry-go-round. Mark watched his family play for a second, and then he sent a text to Leslie asking if she knew what was going on with Jesse. He placed his phone in the center console and sat on a bench to watch the kids play. Leslie never replied.

SOPHIE

Sophie anxiously sat in the waiting room anticipating the latest update about her baby sister. She laid her head on Chris' shoulder and felt him squeeze her hand. He kissed her head and leaned back on her as Leslie paced the hospital floor restlessly and repeatedly peeked around corners, searching for Doctor James. Her heels clacked on the floor as the paced. She tossed her bag on the seat near her, which made a loud bang.

"Mom. Will you please sit down? Watching you pace back and forth is exhausting. They said the doctor will be right out," Sophie barked.

"It's taking too long. It's been almost seven minutes. There is absolutely no urgency in this damn hospital," Leslie snarled.

"They have hundreds of patients to take care of, Mom. I get that you're a newscaster, and your face gets recognized, but you're not the only person here. Lizzie is not the only patient here. Did you know there are five other patients in this burn unit? That's six patients that need round-the-clock, 24/7 care. Six! I hate to say it, but Lizzie isn't the only one. You need to sit your ass down and get a hold of yourself," Sophie lectured. She stormed off to the restroom, leaving Chris in his seat, his mouth on the floor. Leslie shook her head in disgust and plopped into the nearest chair. Awkward silence ensued until the doctor walked down the hallway. Chris motioned to the doctor to wait just a moment for Sophie to reappear.

"The IV treatments are doing well at keeping fluids in Lizzie's body. We are keeping her sedated in her coma so her body can focus on what needs to heal, and there is a consistent drip of morphine going into her system, so she isn't feeling any pain. As you know, she did breathe in a lot of smoke in the accident," Doctor James reported. Sophie started to tear up, since this was the first time she was hearing some of the information. "We have been keeping an eye on her coughing, and she has stopped coughing up blood, which is progress. There is still a big chance she will have breathing problems long-term. We are still looking at the best course of action for her skin. Unfortunately, there isn't enough unburned or undamaged skin to do natural skin grafts, so we are looking at some synthetic alternatives as a temporary fix," Doctor James continued to explain. Leslie shook her head in disapproval.

"Looking at? Temporary fix? Why haven't you done anything yet? My daughter is a vegetable, and your team is just sitting around doing nothing," Leslie barked. Chris's elbow bumped her side to tell her to stop. "I have been here every day and there has been no progress. My daughter has her life ahead of her, and you are taking it away, just like that!"

"Mom, stop!" Sophie jumped in. She stood in between her and the doctor. "I'm sorry, doctor. I know you are doing everything you can with the resources you are given. I thank your team for what you are doing with all your patients. You said synthetic alternatives?" She tried to change the subject. The doctor turned to Sophie and started explaining the process of the alternatives. Eventually, skin grafts will be taken from Lizzie's healed skin to replace the alternatives, but her healing process would take months. Leslie shook her head in disbelief at the explanation and stormed off angrily. Chris stood next to Sophie to have a better ear, and he hugged his wife to comfort her with the overwhelming information she was receiving on behalf of the family. Later that day, they walked back to the car in silence, Chris letting Sophie grasp what she just learned, and Leslie too angry to speak.

HOLLY

Holly and Mark walked into the rental they were staying in temporarily, dropping their bags and keys on the end table and their jackets on the back of the couch. Holly grabbed a couple bottles of water from the fridge and met Mark on the couch. He powered up the TV and checked his phone for work emails. Holly could sense something was up. She nudged his side to get his attention, and she asked what was going on in his mind. Mark sat his cracked phone face-down on the couch and rubbed his hands together, thinking.

"I don't know what to do. I've never been one to jump at the chance to be with the kids. In fact, it's been nice to be without. But this whole debacle is making me think a little more," he admitted. "Seeing Lizzie on that bed…. that killed me."

"Do you think you checked out because of all the trouble Leslie put you through? I know you get sweaty palms when you think about her arriving with the kids, or even talking to her on the phone," Holly suggested while she opened the bottle and handed the water to him. Mark told her it was possible. Their marriage crumbled under the pressures of their fast-paced jobs, turbulent arguments, and different outlooks. Mark explained that it was almost easier to cut the kids out than to deal with the tornado that was their mother. Holly could see Mark's face almost lose his passion, and she suggested that maybe it was time to make a change. Maybe there was a reason for what they were going through.

"What does work think about you being away?" Holly asked.

"I think they're okay with it, under the circumstances. I don't think they like that I'm physically not there, but I don't really have a choice at the moment," he said, lifting his phone to make sure there were no new notifications that needed attending to.

"I think you do have a choice," Holly started. "And I think it says something that you decided to be here." She smiled meekly over at Mark, who shrugged and lost his attention to the high-speed chase ensuing on the TV.

GOOD MORNING

LIZZIE

There's something about medical intervention that can give someone crazy dreams. In my sedated slumber, my entire life played out in my head. It wasn't real life, though. A strange, almost perfect version of my life played itself out. My parents were still together. I graduated high school even earlier than I was already on track to and went on to become a world-renowned pediatrician. My brother went on to be a championship racecar driver. Grandma Faulkner never struggled with dementia, and we were the best of friends. But soon, that dream became a nightmare.

The beautiful, flowery scenes of my family succeeding in everything they did soon transform into flashes of light, screams, and demons flying in and swooping my family away. Suddenly, I was drowning in a pool of flames as ghostly shrieks filled the air. I felt a throbbing in my back, and it felt like my limbs are being pulled apart. I was shaken awake by the horrific nightmare and the heart monitor screaming for the nurses. Gasping for air, I was so agitated from the dream that I attempted to rip away the tubes and straps on my body, with no avail. I could barely move without my skin seemingly crumbling apart and stinging like eight million paper cuts deep into my tissue. The nurse charged in and pleaded with me to relax while she placed more medication into my IV. The sight of another human being miraculously calmed me down and brought me back to earth.

"Please, ma'am. Where am I?" I asked through my burned, chapped lips. The only thing I recognized is the heart monitor. "Where am I? What's going on? Why are all these tubes on me? Why can't I move?"

"Do you really not know where you are?" the nurse asked. My head shook slightly, and I cringed at the pain that followed.

"I feel like I've been asleep for a year and missed everything," I replied curiously.

"Well, my name is Lyla, and I'm your nurse. You are at the hospital. That fire at the elementary school? You pushed a couple of students out of the way of a falling power pole and took the blow yourself. You have some severe burns and breaks in your back, so we've had you in a medically induced coma for about a month, but we are doing our very best to take care of you," she explained. I smiled slightly to try to show I understood, even though I didn't, and I closed my eyes to try to relax.

"Fire? Fire? So… is everyone okay?" I asked Lyla before she exited my room. "Has it really been a month?"

"Yes. There weren't any other casualties. You saved a couple of other children. You were extremely brave," the nurse encouraged me. I heard the door close, and the combination of faint sound of game shows on TV and whatever concoction she placed in my IV seemed to put me back to sleep.

The next morning, I woke up to the doctor talking to Lyla about my vitals. I only had the strength to open one eye to see a tall man in a white coat nodding with a clipboard in his hand. He noticed I was awake and walked over to my side.

"Good morning, Miss Lizzie. Doctor James here. How are you doing this morning?" he asked. I smiled and nodded slightly, cringing at the pain as I continued to learn how much I could take.

"Where is my mom?" I questioned.

"She has come and seen you a couple times since you have been here, but you've been asleep with the coma," the doctor replied. "You seem to be doing a little bit better, so I can call if you would like and let her know you are awake and asking for her." I nodded again a little lighter this time, so it wasn't as painful. He checked the monitors and called one of the nurses in the hallway; he requested her to call Mom. I laid back in my bed and thought to myself, "I wonder if she has been here a lot. I know her. If she is stressed, she's a lot to handle. I hope she hasn't been a lot to handle for these doctors."

SOPHIE

Sophie walked into the nursing home with a little bit of anxiety. She always had a weird feeling about that place, but it was the only place that would take Grandma Faulkner in with the budget they had. She walked down the dark hallway to find the correct room. It had been months since she had made time to see her great-grandmother, but that was a visit she had to make. Life was becoming too much for her to handle, so she ran to the one person that could help her calm down. She walked into the room to see Grandma in her favorite chair looking at her pictures. Grandma heard a sound from the other end of the room, and she turned to see a familiar face.

"Sophie, my baby doll. Come here," she motioned to Sophie to give her a hug. Sophie obliged and kissed her grandmother's head. Her heart melted that she remembered her name. She touched her grandmother's face to feel that familiar comfort and sat on the bed.

"Good morning, Grandma. How are you?" she asked.

"I'm okay. I had chocolate pudding today. Do you know how long it's been since I've had chocolate pudding?" Grandma asked excitedly. Sophie just sat and smiled as her great-grandmother talked about her day. Before the nurse left the room, she whispered to Sophie that chocolate pudding was a daily treat for the residents here. She watched as Grandma picked up a photo from the table and pointed to a face in the scene.

"This is you, right?" she asked. Sophie explained that the face she was pointing at was her mother, and the little girl in the background was her. The picture was taken when everyone was little, so things looked very different. Grandma nodded her head in understanding and continued to look at her pictures. Sophie sat on the bed in silence for a moment to figure out what she wanted to say.

"Grandma, can I ask you a question?" she asked. Grandma nodded in delight, as if her mind reverted to that of a small child. "There has been a lot going on, and the family has been having a tough time. I want to help, but there isn't a lot that I can do. It hurts, because I feel helpless," she explained. She didn't have the heart to explain what happened to Lizzie.

"Sometimes, life does some weird things," Grandma replied, holding another picture. "You can't own what isn't yours. You are in charge of the life you want. It's okay that you want to help the family, but sometimes, it might not be in the cards. Sometimes, all you can do is be there for them." She picked up a tiny boat from the nightstand and felt the wood carvings with her thumbs. "Your great-grandfather carved me this boat when our kids were little. Do you remember the story about the boat?" she asked. Sophie looked at her grandmother a little confused. "In life, we are all in the same storm, but some people have boats, some people have ships, and some people have life rafts. We need to make sure we have a boat or a ship in this storm, so that when the chance comes that we can help, we can carry people out of their rafts." She continued on comparing boats and life rafts until it became quiet rambling. She looked out the window for a moment, and then back at Sophie. "How are you doing today, honey?"

Sophie made conversation with her great-grandmother to keep her talking. She could see Grandma get so excited with every question she asked, even though she would forget which questions she answered a short time later. After talking about boats, childhood stories, and looking at pictures for what seemed like the whole day, Sophie hugged her great-grandmother and kissed her head again to say good-bye. She reflected on the way home what Grandma had told her. She still didn't know what to do, but all she did know was that she needed to make sure she was in a boat.

Sophie got to her car to see a message from her mom saying that Lizzie was awake from her coma. She raced to the hospital as fast as she could. Maybe she would be able to see Lizzie before she fell asleep again. Doctors always said she was doing well, but the only times she was able to see Lizzie was when she was asleep. She walked into the waiting room to see Doctor James standing at the front counter.

"Excuse me, Doctor?" she asked calmly. The doctor flinched; he turned to see Sophie and smiled. Sophie listened as Doctor James greeted her with joy, telling her that she was the nice one of the family, and so much better to deal with than her mother. He apologized for speaking unkindly about her mother, and he asked if there was anything he could do. Sophie asked if there was any way she could see

Lizzie.

"Yes, you may. Your mother left about an hour ago. I can't promise that she will be awake, but you are more than welcome to go back. The only thing we ask is no physical touch. We are still trying to be extra careful to avoid as much infection with Lizzie as we can," he explained. Sophie nodded in understanding and walked back into her baby sister's hospital room. Lizzie's eyes were open, but she looked a little hazy.

"Lizzie?" she asked as she knocked on the door. Lizzie's head turned slightly to see her older sister standing at the foot of her bed.

"Hey," Lizzie replied. "I'd hug but…" she started, eyeing the bandages and equipment all over. "It's good to see you. You missed Mom."

"I heard, and honestly, I'm kind of glad I did," Sophie replied. Lizzie let out a chuckle that made her cough. After a light coughing episode, her body calmed down, and Sophie talked about her visit with Grandma Faulkner. She talked about looking through pictures with her and how happy she was. She mentioned her forgetting the chocolate pudding and how aged her face had become.

"As much as the dementia is worsening, she still is one of the greatest women I will ever meet. I was going to tell her what was going on, but I couldn't bring myself to do it. She doesn't really understand reality much anymore, and that's a lot of stress to put on someone," Sophie explained.

"I don't blame you; I don't know if I would have been able to tell her either," Lizzie agreed. "But then again, she may surprise everyone."

LIZZIE

Endless thoughts circled themselves in my head as I spent the following days in the quiet, sterile hospital room. "I have been asleep for a month? They said there was a fire at the elementary school. I can't even remember getting to school that day. Everything is so hazy." Every move I made felt like someone lit a match and placed it directly on my skin. "And burns? I feel like someone is carving my skin off my body every time I move." The sparse walls in the room continued to remind me how isolated I was. "I guess the nurse had them remove the mirror across the room so I wouldn't be able to see myself? Is it really that bad? Why hasn't Mom been here while I have been awake? Where is she?"

MARK

Mark picked up Jesse from school after receiving a call about another fight. That was the third call about Jesse's behavior just that week. Mark drove to a quiet park on the outskirts of town. There weren't a lot of people around with it being the middle of the day, so there weren't a lot of distractions. He sat Jesse down at a picnic table near the car and placed a pizza in the center of the table. He sat down and looked at Jesse for a moment before he could figure out what to say.

"I'm worried about you Jesse. This is the third call I've had this week. It looks like things are getting worse. What's going on?" he asked with concern. Jesse shrugged his shoulders in silence and looked away, almost feeling ashamed. "Jesse, this is serious. What is going on at home? I know I've been picking you up from school lately and having your mother come to my house to get you, but you're still talking back and starting fights. Tell me Jesse," Mark's voice became very stern. "What is going on? You're making this very hard for everyone, especially with what's going on with…"

"It's always about her!" Jesse yelled. "You were going to say Lizzie, weren't you?! It's always about her. All Mom talks about is her! Lizzie this,

Lizzie that. Doctors are doing this; doctors aren't doing that. She yells at me all night when I get home, but I didn't do anything!" He started to tear up. "I don't matter to this family. I've just been someone to scream at. No one loves me," his young son explained before folding his arms and retreating into himself. Mark's face drooped in defeat over what he just heard. Emotions filled his soul: guilt, realizing he hadn't done his part to make Jesse feel okay; anger towards his ex-wife who was being extremely harsh and neglectful towards their youngest child. "Did she have no emotion at all? What is wrong with this woman?"

"Jesse… I'm so sorry. I didn't know," he replied, shoulders slumped. "This isn't your battle. You should only have to worry about being a kid. You shouldn't have to deal with all this adult stuff. You have done nothing wrong. I will do everything I can to make sure things change. I know you need to be important, too. You know why? Because you are. There has been a lot happening lately, but that is no excuse. I will try my best to change, okay? Just make me a promise, please stop fighting in school… Please… And if you need anything, please tell me," Mark pleaded. Jesse shrugged quietly while he bit down on his next slice of pizza.

After a while, it got windy enough that the boys called it a day and hopped in the car to go home.

They walked into Mark's apartment to find Holly taking cookies out of the oven. She rushed over and hugged Jesse tightly and kissed Mark on the cheek. Jesse ran to the television to pull out the videogame consoles to play. Mark pulled Holly into the corner and told her about the surprise lunch, and the calls from the school. Holly's lips pursed and she clutched her chest when she heard about what Jesse told his father. "The gall of some people to treat their children so harshly. He is a young kid."

"I don't know what to do, Holly. The kid is struggling. We're supposed to be heading back in three days. I haven't told him that we are leaving yet, but we can't go like this," Mark admitted, a rogue tear squeezing out of his eye socket. "Something is telling me we need to be here."

"Mark," Holly said while putting her hands on his shoulders. She shook him slightly to get him to pay attention. "To be honest, I've been thinking about that, too. There is so much crumbling down around us, and I agree with you. We need to be here," she agreed. Mark smiled, and his shoulders slumped.

"What do we do?" he asked.

"All you have to do is figure everything out for work. Do you think the company will let you work from home? I can take care of the rest," Holly replied confidently. He had a sneaking suspicion this was too much confidence, but he hugged his girlfriend and sat on the couch with a couple of cookies to share with Jesse. "God, I love that girl…" he thought to himself. Mark thought about everything that could possibly change in the next few months, but there was one change about Holly he was getting particularly excited about. He spent the next 20 minutes or so quietly watching Jesse play.

"Jesse, what do you think about coming here to live with Holly and me?" he asked out of nowhere. Holly jerked her head in his direction with a shocked look on her face. Jesse dropped everything and stared at his father.

"Mark!" Holly let out.

"Really? Dad really? Wait, really?" Jesse asked elatedly. Mark nodded his head and turned to face Holly as Jesse jumped in his arms. Holly took a moment to register what just happened, and mouthed the word "now?" Mark nodded his head in her direction. He watched Holly rub her forehead in deep thought of the endless list of things to figure out. "I have to talk to your mom, but things are going to change whether she likes it or not. They need to," Mark commented. Jesse released his grip and looked at his father defeatedly. Seeing Jesse's reaction to the mention of his mother, Mark repeated, "I promise."

MARK

"You are not taking my son, you son of a bitch!" Leslie screamed at Mark over the phone. Mark explained what happened at the park and what Jesse said. He reminded her of a conversation he had with Kris, and her opinions about her. "I am a good mother; do you hear me? You are not taking my son! Just because the doctors piss me off does not give you the right to take him away!" she continued to berate. "Kris is a no-good, slimy slob that doesn't deserve that house, or that money!"

"Leslie, stop!" Mark commanded. "You're validating my case by leaving our son with a woman even you have horrid feelings for! He is my son, too. I can't help that you haven't been answering the calls from the school, but the kid is suffering. You can't sit there and scream at him! He did nothing! You hear me? Nothing! How dare you?" he continued to scream. Leslie continued to scream about Lizzie's doctors and Sophie no longer contacting her. Mark could hear the defeat in her voice, as she realized slowly her ex-husband was telling her that her son was leaving. The fight became more hostile, as Leslie and Mark went back and forth about their failed marriage and each other's faults, attacking each other's throats until someone waved a white flag.

"The decision is done, Leslie. I am not changing my mind, and Jesse already knows the plan. You can spend all the attention you want on your precious little job and apparently your only child," Mark stated before hanging up the phone. He wiped the sweat off his forehead and grabbed a bottle of water to soothe his inflamed throat. He sat on the couch and reflected on the situation until Holly brought Jesse home from school. Things could have been said differently, but when emotions ran high, all bets were off on either side. Just one of the many faults that resulted in their divorce.

A few days later, Mark and Holly finished packing their belongings to move into the new rental Holly had found with lucky timing. They had planned to get their belongings to the new house, and then Mark was going to take Jesse on a road trip to their apartment in the city to grab some more things to move to the rental. Mark thought this was the perfect time to spend his attention only on Jesse, trying to make him feel happier since the accident.

Jesse ran and skipped around the apartment complex lawn until he couldn't breathe. Being in a new environment and away from the drama excited him, and he couldn't wait to discover something new and thrilling. Mark watched his son gallop with glee around the yard, letting himself be free from the pain that was going on at home. He relaxed his mind briefly, feeling and hoping like he was giving his son something different to help him cope with everything that was happening. He walked to the door and opened the entrance to his humble, ultra-modern abode, and ushered Jesse inside. As Jesse ran around the house feeling and touching all the decorations, Mark was in his room packing up some more belongings to take back to the rental: his laptop, more clothes, Holly's special shampoo, etc. He placed everything on the bed and grabbed the suitcase behind the door. He ran through his head the list that Holly had given him, before opening the refrigerator to give Jesse something to drink.

"You look really happy right now. Are you having fun?" he asked his rambunctious child.

"This…is…so…COOOL! How long are we going to be here? Can we get burgers? What is it like to live here? Are you rich?" Jesse rambled on and on. Mark hugged his son tightly as he continued to blast off question after question, not giving him a chance to answer any of them. He just smiled and let Jesse continue until he collapsed on the couch in exhaustion from all the excitement. Mark turned on the television to distract him for a bit while he finished packing the suitcase. The last item to go in was a suspicious little box, packed deep in one of the side pockets.

Mark drove Jesse around the city all day, stopping frequently to let him see the sights, run around the parks, letting him be a kid. He took pictures of Jesse with a superhero that was walking around the sidewalk, showed him the building where he worked, and he raced him up the flights of steps like the movie Rocky. It wasn't Philadelphia, but close enough. After getting Jesse some ice cream, they sat on a bench next to the lake for some calm resting time. Jesse scarfed down the ice cream as if he hadn't eaten in years, and he sat watching the ducks on the lake until he passed out in his father's lap. Mark stayed still for a few minutes to make sure Jesse was sound asleep, and then he carried him to the car. He drove to a truck stop on the outside of town to grab some burgers as a surprise to Jesse for later, and he continued on the quiet trip back home. Mark smirked a little as he peeked at his sleeping son, feeling like he might have given his son the best day ever, something that this little boy desperately needed. He called Holly and let her know he was on the way home, talking just above a whisper as to not wake him up.

BURDEN

LIZZIE

Each and every day dragged on in this hospital. I was continuing to heal and become stronger, but every treatment they did for my skin brought me back to all that pain, the only thing I remembered from the accident. Some days, I just wished the pain would stop. I didn't want to do it anymore. I wanted for the pain to suck the life out of my body and let me die. Other days, I championed that pain and willed my body to fight to heal. It had been a continuous roller coaster of painful treatments, more skin grafts, and pain medication. It has been a journey of trying to register what was happening in my new normal life. Mom hadn't come to the hospital as often, and from the sounds of the doctor's voice when I overheard him talking about it, he was okay with it. "I get it; Mom is a lot sometimes, even for me. I just wish she was here, though. Where is Mom? I just want my mom."

I remembered when I was little, Mom would always tell us to "Fight for our dreams" and "Don't take no for an answer." She did that every day of her life. I think the "Don't take no for an answer" part, however, kind of gave her an ego though, especially when it came to the promotion she got at work. She was now the head newscaster on screen, a personality that would now get noticed in public everywhere we went. She got the attention she craved, I guess. I remembered hearing her and Dad fighting about that a lot before they got divorced. Dad was working long, long hours, but Mom expected him to give her the same amount of attention, regardless of if it was an eight-hour shift or 14. I love my mom to death, and sometimes she was the coolest mom ever, but even as a kid, I felt that was a little unfair for her to expect that from Dad. They finally split up right after Jesse was born.

Mom and Dad kept the divorce pretty quiet. Dad simply left. We woke up one day, and it was like he didn't exist. Sophie was angry for a long time. She was older than I was, so she understood more of what happened, and she took it harder than the rest of us. I was just really confused. I understood why she was so angry the older I got. They were supposed to be together forever.

As I reminisced to myself, the 1,000th episode of the next game show on TV announced that the winning prize was a massive houseboat. Not like "I'm the CEO" completely massive, but bigger than most ski-boats. It threw me back to the last time I went to visit Grandma Faulkner. It was out of nowhere when she began to lecture me about the struggles of the world and being able to make sure I had a boat so I could pull people out of the water. My heart broke from this memory. There I was in a hospital bed, completely helpless, and my family had to pick up the pieces and try to figure out what was happening. My boat crashed, and I was floating on a door, while my family was trying to desperately get their life jackets on. I missed Grandma. I know it had been a couple months since I had seen her, but not a day went by that I hadn't thought about her.

When she lived with us, there was always a bet as to who could get their chores done first or a race to the couch to watch her show. The amount of ice cream sandwiches she snuck us when Mom wasn't home could make an igloo in the middle of the living room, where she would always encourage us to throw pillow fights or destroy the furniture making the most advanced fort possible. She never went to sleep without her evening cuddles on the couch and telling endless stories of how she grew up and what life had taught her. Over the years, the stories became more scatterbrained; some days, she wouldn't really make a lot of sense. Occasionally, she would start to switch our names around. The hardest part was watching her body slowly forget how to take care of itself. She started to move around slower, and she would forget to eat for a day or two. Sometimes, I would walk out of my room at night to grab a glass of water just in time to see Mom cleaning up after Grandma when she started to have accidents more often. It wasn't long after that, Mom sent her to a nursing home. She never really liked taking us to see her, either. She always acted like it was somewhat of a burden.

LIZZIE

Nurse Lyla came in to check on the IVs. We had some short talk about the weather and new shows on TV (that unfortunately I couldn't watch). I tried my best to maneuver myself in the bed, to no avail. The scraping sensation on my skin was almost too much, but I realized again that I couldn't move my legs. My brows furrowed with confusion, but the color left my face as I started to realize that I couldn't get them to come back to life.

"Uhmmmm… Lyla?" my voice shook as I tried voraciously to move the lower half of my body. Lyla saw the worry and fear in my face. She told me to relax, and she would get the doctor. "Why can't I move my legs?!"

A few moments later, Lyla ran back in, followed by Doctor James. He asked how I was doing, but the answer broadcasted itself with the fear in my face.

"I heard that you noticed you can't feel your legs," he said awkwardly, pulling up a chair to the side of the bed. "I think it's time that you know what exactly you have been dealing with." I felt the color further drain from my face, fear taking over my body. Lyla walked over to the other side of my bed, placing her hand on my blankets covering my stomach, as if to keep me from sitting up more. "When the power pole fell, it snapped a few vertebrae in your back; it also did damage to your spinal cord, which has unfortunately paralyzed you from the waist down." He paused for a moment to let me take in what I just heard. I couldn't say anything. Tears welled up in my eyes.

"I.... I'm paralyzed?" I repeated back. That moment didn't feel real. Was this really happening?

"Lizzie," Doctor James cleared his throat. "We've also been taking care of extreme burns to your skin, which you have been aware of," he continued, almost in a sarcastic tone as if to lighten up the moment. I nodded in agreement.

"How could I not be aware of that?" I answered snarkily. My eyes rolled while the doctor continued. My breathing got heavier as the reality of the situation started to seep in.

"The reality is, with all the grafts, therapy, and treatments you may need, there is a high chance you may be here for a while... a long while.... Uhmmmm.... I'm sorry. I know that's the last thing you want to hear, but we are going to take good care of you, okay?" his presentation ended. I couldn't move. My brain couldn't comprehend anything I just heard. Questions like. "I'm paralyzed? How long is a long while?" screamed in my head and all I could hear in the background was, "waaa, waaa, waaaa, waaa" Doctor James asked if I was okay or if I had any other questions. It took a moment before I was able to snap back enough to know exactly what he asked. I looked around and asked why the mirror was taken out of the room. I had never seen that done in a hospital before. Lyla braced herself at the foot of the bed.

"I requested to have that removed. I wanted you to focus on healing. I thought that seeing your face right now might scare you, because you do look very different," she explained slowly. My brows furrowed in confusion. My stomach dropped. I asked how different, only to be met by Lyla looking concerned towards Doctor James. He had his hand on his chin for a moment as he thought, then he nodded his head. Lyla reluctantly dragged her feet towards the corner of the room to pick up a hand mirror that sat on the counter. She brought it to the side of the bed and asked if I was ready. Still confused, I nodded my head, and she held the mirror in front of my face.

I didn't recognize myself anymore. This wasn't the same person, was it? A large patch of burned skin trailed from the side of my chin to just above my left eye. Another scar was forming across my forehead, cutting off my right eyebrow, and catching on my ear. The rest of my face was red and blistered in places. I looked like a monster. My breath hastened, and tears started to flow uncontrollably from my eyes. In the background, I heard my heart monitor start screaming. Lyla quickly took the mirror away and grabbed towels and gauze to wipe the salty tears away from my scarred face, and Doctor James jumped up to check the monitors.

"I think that's enough for today," Doctor James nervously suggested. Lyla nodded her head and mentioned she would stay to make sure I calmed down. Doctor James left the room; Lyla sat on the seat he had left, still dabbing the tears off my face. She tried saying that she didn't want me to find out like this, and how sorry she was that it overwhelmed me so much, only to see me stressing even more. In between heavy breaths, I tried to yell as loud as I could, "I can't walk? I'm an invalid now? Does Mom know? I'm going to be a burden to her. What am I going to do?" Quiet, breathy words came out instead. Lyla tried to ask me to calm down, that the talking would exhaust my lungs. "And I look like a fucking monster. I'm never going to be able to go anywhere. I can't show my face again! I can't let Jesse see this. Never! I'd be better off dead or never have existed." Endless tears poured from my face. Lyla called another nurse in because she couldn't keep up.

"Please help me," she asked. "We can't let these tears irritate her skin." She and this other nurse blotted at my face with gauze after gauze after gauze until I eventually cried myself to sleep.

LIZZIE

I had been in this hospital bed for about a month and a half now. I couldn't tell you for sure; every day blended into one another after a while, especially when one is confined to one small space. I wish I could just walk around: walk around the halls, walk up to the window in my room to look outside, or just get out of bed. I never thought in my wildest dreams that I would end up paralyzed from the waist down. I was 17 years old. School doesn't teach that when helping us with our 10-year plans. I was so far behind in school at that point, there was no way I could graduate early, if even at all. How was my life going to change when I finally got out of there? I still could barely move because of how painful and sensitive my skin was, and I was confined to a wheelchair; that was, when I eventually got out of this bed. I, once fiercely independent, depended on complete strangers for the tiniest of daily tasks. It was humiliating.

It had been so hard to stay present. I still couldn't comprehend what happened in the accident and how it led me there. I stared at my still-healing hands and my patchy stomach, seeing an inhuman creature that crawled out of someone's chest in a scary movie. I was terrified to look in a mirror to see what my face looked like since that first time. Lyla kept saying I looked great and that my body took the worst of it, but I knew better. My brain couldn't handle what I looked like. I just wanted to be home. I wanted to have weird conversations with Jesse. I wanted to be back at school being a normal person. Actually, I didn't. I was disgusting. No one was going to love me. I wanted to disappear.

They were talking about moving me to another floor of the hospital, though. I had been in the ICU since I had been there, but I guess they were talking about sending me to another rehabilitation floor since I had been able to breathe on my own, and

I was more conscious. Too bad I couldn't just go home.

Sophie came in a few days ago. She talked about visiting Grandma Faulkner. I had wished I could have been there with her. Grandma was doing well, but the dementia was slowly getting worse. If I wasn't already feeling helpless, hearing the state she was in and not being able to help her made it worse. Some days I wanted to give up. I was done. I didn't want to feel the pain, I didn't want this helpless feeling. Everything kept crashing down, and it felt like I was continually being sucked into a tornado that I couldn't get out of.

That day when Sophie came in was one of those days. I could tell she felt defeated. "Same girl. Same." I could tell she felt helpless, too. She's trying to clean up everybody's mess and trying to keep our mother from destroying the house, the hospital, everything. She was trying to be the superhero, and I could tell she was getting tired. I looked up to her so much. I never wanted to be a burden to her, but that was all I felt like at that moment. A burden. A vegetable.

"It fucking sucks that nurses have to come in and turn my body every few hours, so I don't develop sores on my barely healing skin," I complained. "The pain has gotten so bad that I have to bite down on towels every time because my skin feels like it's coming off with the blanket. I can't even get up to go to the bathroom." Sophie listened patiently and let me ramble. I told her how I felt trapped and constricted in a shell of what I used to be. I told her how I could almost hear the crinkling of my skin when physical therapists came in to stretch and work my limbs. I shook from the adrenaline and tried to catch my breath. Lyla heard the commotion and came in to check on me, dabbed some rogue tears from my cheeks, and left the room, giving us our privacy. I stared at the wall and listened as Sophie talked, and I just wished over and over again that she didn't have to fight that battle. I wished she didn't have to see me weak and suffering. To some extent, I wished she would leave the hospital and let me be alone.

I had spent hours at a time here alone. Alone in my thoughts. Alone with the sounds of random game shows playing on repeat. Alone with that damn heart monitor that screamed when I blinked. Thank God for Lyla, one of the only people that talked to me when they came in. At least somebody knew I existed, even though I wished they didn't. Physical therapists almost acted like I was another number, another room to appear in and check off. Doctor James was okay, but he always had a habit of being cold. Lyla would at least come in and try to make me feel alive. Yesterday, she came in and played cards on her lunch break. Granted, she had to hold my cards too, but it meant a lot that she was just there. My brain hurt. I wanted so much for everyone to forget about me and let me die, but I couldn't help but want someone there. I just wished I could stop feeling... Just let me stop feeling.

I hadn't seen Dad at all since I'd been in the hospital. I didn't remember ever seeing Jesse; I think Mom didn't bring him because of what I looked like. It would probably traumatize him, which I completely understood. I couldn't look at myself. Half the time when she was here, she was arguing with the doctor and then venting to me about what they were or weren't doing. I missed the days when she was racing through the streets like an action movie. This new person she had become worried me. I just want my mom here. Where was the mom I knew?

There was something about the way she expected things to be done and the newfound entitlement that I didn't like. I just wanted Mom to be here, but it was almost like it was a chore to come see me. Something was different about her since the accident. She had been so much more unpredictable and egotistical with a non-existent fuse. I was not the only one in the hospital, and I knew that, but she expected me to be miraculously healed and everyone to bend down to her to make it happen. It wasn't reasonable for any doctor to focus only on me when there were so many other people that needed help, too. I wished she could sit down and just be with me. Stop yelling at the doctors and nurses. Forget about the assumed lack of care I was getting, and just be here. It would make this dark and depressing hospital room not so prison-like. It had been so hard, having lived a life that was so busy with school and getting ready to graduate, and now I couldn't even get out of bed to use the bathroom. I felt like I was becoming even more invisible to everyone, even to my own mother. I was just a pawn in her games. Nothing but a pawn. "What do I do now? Every single day that passes by, I'm just a burden to everyone. What's the point?"

Nevertheless, there I laid, for the probably 37th day in a row, as helpless and in pain as I was day one. I decided that burn unit time added 10 days to every real day that exists. 370 days…. Sounded about right. No one knew how long I would be in here. I didn't know; the nurses and Doctor James didn't know. No one. I was tired of existing.

Forward

LESLIE

"That is all for tonight folks. We'll see you at nine," Leslie said cheerfully into the camera to close out the segment. She set down her copy about the latest news about the elementary school repairs and walked to her dressing room. She sat down at the desk and stared at the bags that developed under her eyes from the last month and a half of stress, panic, and tragedy that she endured. She put her head in her arms and just tried to breathe. She never thought life would ever have to be this hard. She dreaded having to go to the hospital again, seeing her crippled daughter struggling, and dealing with a doctor that didn't care about her concerns. She hated going home to a quiet house, where she lived alone since Jesse moved in with his "evil, manipulative" father. Life had taken a turn for the worse, and she didn't like it.

"Are you doing okay?" the intern asked. "Boss said I was tasked with following you around for the next couple weeks for job shadowing." He awkwardly stood in the doorway while Leslie fumbled with the papers on her desk trying to find her powder to touch up with.

"Look, kid, I'm fine. Will you leave the room? Maybe shadow the cameraman for a minute?" she asked heatedly. She laid her head back in her hands as he clumsily walked out of the room. Tears started streaming down her face as she finally broke from the pressure of juggling motherhood, this job, the grief of not being able to help her daughter, and her son moving away. She messaged her boss that she was leaving, packed up her purse, and walked away from set. She drove the couple hours to the care home in silence. It was the only place she could think of to go. She needed to get away from the world for a moment.

"Hi Gamm," Leslie blurted out as she walked into her bedroom. Silence followed as Leslie noticed that the room was clean, empty, not lived in. Her heart started to shatter as one of the caregivers passed by.

"Wait! Wait. Where is my grandma? This was her room," she explained.

"I'm sorry ma'am," the caregiver started to explain. "We tried to call you." Leslie's heart dropped to her stomach. Her legs became weak, and she held on to the wall for support. "We did move her to another section of the facility. Her room is this way," Leslie almost collapsed in relief before the caregiver led her to the new room. It was in an area of the facility where patients were looked after a little more closely, which meant the dementia had gotten worse enough that she needed more care. The sight of her grandmother's face made Leslie break down into tears.

"Gamm, I can't do this anymore. Life has been a load of, for the lack of a better word, bullshit, lately, and I'm done," she poured out of her soul. She sat on the bed next to her grandmother and put her hand on her lap.

"Honey, what's the matter?" the bewildered matriarch asked as she put her arms around a tearful Leslie.

"Lizzie was in an accident. She's in the hospital and will never be able to walk anymore, but I don't think the doctors are doing what they can. And Jesse went to live with Mark. Sophie stopped talking to me. I have no one to go home to anymore. I'm all alone, helpless, and nothing seems to be giving in. I can't do anything right, let alone anything to relieve any of this pain," she continued to confess. Leslie felt Gamm's hand stroke her cheek and wipe away a tear as she kissed the top of her head. It was the first feeling of comfort she had felt since the accident.

"I've been through some hard times like you have. Life isn't fair to a lot of people," Gamm explained. "Sometimes we have no idea why things happen, but there is a reason why they do. There is a reason why the accident occurred for Lizzie. There's a reason you've been seeing so much heartache in your life. We don't know what the reason is right now, but eventually we will see it." Gamm continued to just hold Leslie in her arms as she melted down and grieved the pain she hadn't let herself feel until then. The pain and injustice of the last couple months poured out of her body faster than Niagara Falls. She cried until she could no longer breathe. Gamm continued to stay silent as Leslie felt her pain.

"Everything WILL be okay," Gamm encouraged Leslie. She guided Leslie's chin so they were looking eye to eye, and she let out a small, promising smile from her lips. Leslie's head fell back into Gamm's lap as she continued to sob.

"Why does it have to hurt so bad?" she asked in between breaths.

"Some days, I wonder that as well, but it's

only temporary. You can, and you will find your way through this," Gamm explained. She patted the back of an inconsolable Leslie and just let her pour out her emotions for what seemed like hours. One of the caregivers came in to see what the noise was about, and Gamm ushered them away so she and Leslie could continue to be alone. Gamm held Leslie's free hand while the other wiped away a steady stream of tears pouring down her face. Her makeup was destroyed, but that didn't matter anymore. Leslie didn't want to leave this, but she knew eventually she needed to. She tried to breathe as much as she could.

Leslie woke up 2 hours later with Gamm looking at pictures at the nearby desk. Gamm looked over and saw Leslie stirring, and she smiled to see her granddaughter awake.

"I'm still here?" Leslie asked in bewilderment.

"You cried yourself to sleep, darling," Gamm explained. She tidied Leslie's hair as she sat up and wiped her face. "You needed the rest." Her sweet smile comforted Leslie.

"Thank you for being here, Gamm. I'm sorry I poured all this on you," Leslie apologized.

"Don't be sorry. We all need to be comforted when life seems to go awry," Gamm explained. She handed Leslie a photo of her as a child with her mother. Tears started to squeeze out of Leslie's eyes.

"I remember when your mother died like it was yesterday," Gamm said. "There may be things I don't remember anymore, but someone doesn't forget burying a child. I didn't think I would ever get past it. My life was destroyed in one fell swoop. It took me weeks to get out of bed again. It took months for me to get out and live life again. It needed to happen, Leslie. As much as we need to feel our emotions, we can't dwell on the pain we endured. I needed to remember there were still people that needed me. We must learn how to move forward and become stronger." Gamm wiped away the tears sliding down Leslie's face. "Your mom wouldn't want this for you. I don't want this for you. Your children wouldn't want this for you. Please, take time for yourself and gather your thoughts about what this life will hold for you now, okay?" she pleaded with Leslie. Leslie nodded her head and smiled at her wise grandmother, handing the picture back to her.

Leslie took the journey home in silence. A sense of relief washed over her as she had given herself time to release her emotions, but there was still a heavy cloud over her head. Lizzie was still in the hospital, and Jesse was still with his father. "What do I need to do to fix this? Why did this have to happen to me?" she questioned herself repeatedly as she travelled down the long, narrow highway. Navigating a new normal didn't make sense as her brain continued to try to comprehend what Gamm said. "I am now supposed to take time for myself and figure out what life holds? How?"

Leslie walked into the front door, with the only sound in the house being the refrigerator dropping ice. Complete silence. She missed the sound of Jesse slamming his backpack on the floor as he ran into the house from the school bus, even though he never put his backpack away. She missed watching Lizzie play with her little brother and teaching him more about the world. Leslie laid in bed to try to rest, clutching onto the nearest pillow for comfort to protect her from the vulnerable thoughts inside her head. She fell asleep to the sound of the AC blowing air into the room, thinking. Just thinking.

Over the next few days, Leslie let herself stay in bed all day. She called in to work and stated she was going on leave, and she pulled the covers over her head again. She walked out of the bedroom only to open the fridge and decide whether she wanted to eat or not. Most of the time, the answer was no. With no one else home, the house was too big. She couldn't take the space. She locked herself in her room as much as she could, and her only human contact was a random text from Sophie or Jessie replying to her check-ins… Life became… mind-numbing to Leslie. "How do I move forward?"

LIZZIE

"Are you enjoying being out of the ICU?" Lyla asked me as she put down her card. She transferred departments when I moved, just so she could keep me company. Playing cards on her lunch break had become a part of our daily schedule.

"Uhmmmm yes…. Even though most of my time was spent alone anyways, it does feel nice that I'm not being checked on every 4 hours," I replied as I pointed to a card for her to set down. "It's weird though. I haven't seen Mom for a while. Do you think she's okay?"

"I'm sure she's fine," Lyla smiled. "What are you thinking about?"

"A lot of it is wondering what's happening at home. I haven't seen anyone other than my sister lately, and it's out of character for my family. And I'm kind of missing my great grandma a lot. It's been so long since I last saw her," I explained.

"She is in the assisted living center across town, right?" Lyla asked curiously.

"Ya, from the sounds of it, she was just moved to the memory care and dementia wing not too long ago. Why?" I asked. Lyla explained she had a friend that worked there and would talk about this lady that constantly looked at her pictures and told such imaginative stories about life. "That sounds like her, alright." I was so happy to hear she was doing well. I wished I could see her in person. I didn't know if I could handle her seeing what I look like, though. I was finally able to look in the mirror again and see that half my face was practically gone. I looked like I could play a character in the Phantom of the Opera. I would probably be the devilish antagonist or something like that. I looked like a monster. The one that hid in the shadows and only came out to sing about the anger of being rejected, and then hiding myself away again. I probably would not end up with a dude at the end because: 1-I was 17, which would probably cause some legal issues; and 2- I looked terrifying. "Who would fall in love with this? Who would want someone that was damaged and scarred like this?"

I had a random visitor come to the hospital yesterday. The one and only Ms. Wesley showed up with flowers and to check on me. The look of shock when she first walked in and saw what had become of my face only added to the newfound self-confidence issues. Lyla whispered in my ear that I looked fine, and that she was just being dramatic. It didn't help.

Ms. Wesley sat with me for an entire afternoon and caught me up on what was going on. The school is still closed until further notice while they work on the repairs and the remodel. STEM had been canceled, so she had a little bit taken off her plate. We talked about how much I wanted to be back in school and how far behind I had become. She sat for the longest time telling me how incredible I was and how confident she was that I would catch up in no time when I got back. She cheered in excitement as she explained how much help I had been to her, and how much power she saw in my work ethic and ability to catch on quickly. The only thing I could do was sit and listen, smiling at what she saw in me. Occasionally, I saw Lyla in the background nodding in agreement with whatever Wesley was saying. I felt better for a moment, but all my thoughts continued to come back to reality, where I probably wouldn't be able to work with little kids anymore.

LIZZIE

Lyla woke me up the next morning to check and make sure I was still okay. My dinner tray was still on the table nearby, untouched. It was the first night that I got more than a couple hours of sleep, so it took me a solid minute to figure out which decade I woke up in. Once I finally came to, I had to beg her for food because I was absolutely starving. I still was not able to eat too much, but I needed something in my stomach. Life was too exciting to starve now. I had to tell Lyla about everything that happened yesterday afternoon, at least the parts that she missed. It was the first day in a long time that I felt like a weight was lifted off of me. It inspired me to keep going and get better. I may have looked like a nightmare, but maybe life itself didn't have to be that way.

Lyla had to interrupt me and remind me that she was there. I was still so excited; I couldn't stop talking anyways. She told me she had a surprise, and I stopped in my tracks. She got paid to take care of me, not give me surprises. She told me she had talked to her friend who worked at the nursing home. She looked down and started tapping her phone, and before I knew it, I was face to face with Grandma Faulkner. I started to cry immediately when I saw one of the loves of my life waving back at me. After watching the camera for a moment to figure out what was happening with this newfound technology, she blew a kiss at me, and I blew one back. She didn't react the way most people had reacted to the scars on my face, which shocked me. Grandma didn't have a face that kept quiet.

"How are you doing sweet girl?" Grandma asked me.

"I'm doing okay Grandma, how are you?" I replied while choking back tears. The past 24 hours had been a roller coaster of emotions, and then this?

"Did you know that I can see you through this phone? How amazing are the times now?" she blurted out excitedly, amazed at the advancements in modern technology. I watched as I saw her hands feel the phone and watched her look into the phone as if there was something she was trying to find. Her fingers poked at the screen.

"I'm so happy to see you Grandma!" I said.

"Baby, I love you so much. You look as beautiful as ever," she commented. I continued to sob at her sweet words, and my heart melted just seeing her smile.

"Grandma, these scars make me nauseous. You didn't react the way everyone has reacted when they saw my face for the first time. Did they not shock you?" I questioned.

"Sweetie, the only face I see is the face of my great-granddaughter. The only thing different is how much you have grown since I last saw you!" she replied encouragingly. We talked for probably an hour as she learned how to show me pictures on the phone, and I talked about how Ms. Wesley came up yesterday and what being in the hospital was like.

"I think you can still graduate early," she mentioned excitedly.

"Do you think so? I've missed a lot," I confess. "I don't even know when I will be able to go back to school."

"You are smart. You've always been so smart and learned so fast. I know you will do great things," she encouraged me. The nurse dabbed away tears streaming down my face as my heart melted listening to her being so sweet.

"Grandma, have you heard from Mom? I haven't seen her for a while," I asked.

"I saw her not too long ago, sweetie. She was having a hard day, but she was okay when she left," she answered. There was a confused tone to her voice, so both of us were apparently unaware that my mother has just disappeared out of nowhere.

"I'm sure she's busy with work. I think Sophie is coming up soon. I can ask her as well," I mentioned. I did NOT want to stress Grandma out more. Grandma had to go take her medication, so we ended the call. Lyla patted my head lightly and helped get me to my side. I was especially achy after the move, so she gave me some pain medication and walked out of the room. Where was Mom? Why had she not come up lately? I wonder what Dad was doing. I hoped Jesse was doing okay. Where was everybody?

BIRTHDAY

SOPHIE

Sophie and Chris drove up to the park in anticipation. It was Jesse's birthday and had also been a few weeks since Jesse moved in with Mark. They were still struggling with him fighting at school, so Sophie's nerves ramped up, as she didn't know if his anger would come out towards her kids. It hadn't yet, but there were so many unknowns. They ran out of the car faster than a hurricane, and Jesse knocked over the stack of cups as he jumped from the picnic table to meet them. All the kids piled on top of each other in celebration, emanating such child-like joy that the adults couldn't help but smile. Sophie's nerves subsided seeing her little brother greet her kids with such delight. They gave the kids permission to go run around the playground, while they sat around the picnic table to catch up.

"So, while the kids are gone, Lizzie is doing

really well. She is healing well, and they moved her from the ICU," Sophie explained to Mark. Mark nodded his head in approval. "There's something that is bothering me though…. I don't know if she's been showing up when Lizzie was asleep, but Lizzie doesn't remember her being there. She's stopped texting back anything other than short replies to text messages. I guess Lizzie was able to video chat with Grandma a while ago, and the last time Grandma saw Mom, she was an emotional wreck. I'm kind of worried about her," Sophie continued to explain.

"I have noticed the same thing when we check Jesse's phone," Holly replied. "I know we got that so he could have contact with Leslie, but the communication has to work both ways. I don't know how to change that." Mark shrugged with dismissal.

"I'm sure she's okay. I know I don't get along with her, but one thing I do know is that she's a strong son of a…" Mark started when Holly elbowed his side. "What I'm saying is, she may just be handling things her way. Give it time." He dug into the bag of chips on his right and started munching.

"It's weird, you know? I've never experienced her this way," Sophie replied. Chris held her hand as she explained how Leslie had changed over the past few months: the outbursts, the arguments. She started telling stories of the mother that raised her, a completely different woman than who she was currently seeing.

"I just wish I could help. I don't want her to hurt, but I feel like anything I do isn't changing or helping anything," she explained, tears starting to well in her eyes. Holly breathed in to begin to speak, and then Mark straightened himself.

"Soph, listen to me, okay?" he asked. "Look at me. This is not your battle to fight. It's not. I can understand that she is your mother, and you care and worry about her as I do you, but there comes a point where you do need to back up and care about yourself and your own family. You have a supportive husband and 3 young kids that need you in their lives. Don't let this swallow you, Sophie, okay?" Mark lectured. "This is not your battle to fight." Sophie sat up and cleared her throat, choking back tears. She asked how Jesse was doing and how he was adjusting to the move. Holly kicked in and started explaining how the fights had decreased, but they were still getting weekly calls from the school about him speaking out or misbehaving. He started having a lack of being able to pay attention in class and keeping him in from recess wasn't helping. She mentioned he is the perfect kid at home, so they were still trying to figure out why he was so different in school. Her updates were cut off by a hoard of small children running up to ask if it was time for cake and presents.

All the kids jumped up onto the table and started to grab plates and forks and lining up for cake. Holly ushered Jesse to sit in front of the cake so they could sing Happy Birthday. After singing, Jesse paused to wish, and then blew out his candles. Mark threw himself over the cake before the kids destroyed the evidence. After all the adults finally got the kids to calm down and sit in their places, Mark cut the cake into pieces and served it onto everybody's plates. Life continued in silence for a good five minutes while the kids indulged themselves with all the sugar they could eat. The adults eyed each other at the table, smiling about the fact that it was so quiet with this rambunctious set of children. Of course, Jesse was the first one done with his cake. With confidence, he held his plate high in the air and declared he was the world champion of cake eating, and that he was now ready for his birthday presents.

"Ey boy, good job!" Chris stated. "The rest of us need to finish, too."

"Eat faster, boyyyy!" Jesse snarkily responded. Mark gave Jesse permission to go back to the playground and play, and a couple of the kids followed not long after. After everyone else finished, and after a quick bathroom break for Sophie and her youngest, Mark started yelling in an absurd, siren-like voice to announce that it was now present time. The army of children rushed to the scene, and everyone was ushered to sit in a circle in the grass near the picnic table. Present after present, Jesse jumped and yelled with excitement for the toy foam guns, army men, new clothes, and a new skateboard from his dad that he viciously unwrapped himself. Sophie's children cheered with excitement, and they all started grabbing at the gifts to help Jesse un-package them to play. The wide-eyed adults sprang into action and attempted to explain that the option to play with all the small toys now wasn't an option due to the high chance of losing pieces, only to have protesting children throwing the toys back into a pile.

As the children lost attention and ran to the swings to continue to play, Holly and Sophie sat under the shade of a nearby maple tree. Sophie sat with her knees folded up to her chest, watching her precious children decide who was going to be the captain of the imaginary pirate ship they created. Holly asked Sophie how she was holding up, scratching her back to comfort her. Sophie rested her folded arms on her knees and laid her head across them, looking at Holly. She sighed, pausing for a moment to think.

"To be honest, I don't really know. Everything keeps spinning so fast, I feel like I can't grip onto anything." Holly leaned over and hugged Sophie, whispering in her ear that everything would be okay. They continued to sit and watch the young pirates collect their treasures of pinecones and small twigs in a pile under the slide. Jesse ran up behind the ladies and startled them, making Sophie and Holly jump feet into the air. He sat between the 2, leaning his back against the tree.

"How's your birthday, bud?" Sophie asked.

"It was the best! Thank you for all the presents!" he replied, looking at both Holly and Sophie repeatedly. His little body bounced up and down as he explained his plans for the military men and toy foam guns. Mark called Holly over to the car, so she left Sophie and Jesse sitting by the tree. Jesse leaned his head on his big sister's shoulder.

"I miss Lizzie," he admitted. Sophie put her arm around his back and squeezed tight.

"You've never gone this long without seeing Lizzie, have you?" she asked. Jesse shook his head. "Lizzie missed you, too. One of these days, I'm sure Dad and Holly will be able to take you. I'm sure she would love to see you. She talks about you a lot." Jesse's eyes beamed; he mouthed "really?" to Sophie, who nodded her head in return. Sophie mentioned that he had to stop fighting in school, and do his best to be better, if not for him, then for Lizzie. Jesse's demeanor dropped a little. He agreed and leaned back to his sister's side. She put her arm around her baby brother, and they sat under the tree watching the rest of their family enjoy the afternoon. Even though there was so much Sophie couldn't control or fix, she appreciated this small moment to love and comfort her brother.

MARK

"Hi, Mom! Today was so cool! We went to the park, had cake, and opened soooo many presents! I got a giant toy foam gun and so many army men to use as targets! Sophie was there! Holly was there! I wish you were there. I do miss you. You should text me. Bye!" was the message Jesse left when he called his mother on the way home from the party at the park. He hadn't seen his mom since he moved in with Mark and Holly, and Leslie's texts were getting shorter and shorter. His shoulders slumped in defeat.

"Did Mom forget about me?" he asked.

"Of course, she didn't, Jesse," Holly replied quickly. "She could never forget about her only son. She has a lot going on, but I promise, she did not forget about you, and she loves you very much." Mark peeked in the rear-view mirror to see Jesse's reaction, who was now looking through the window, his lips pursed on one side of his face as he was in deep thought. He turned the radio to Jesse's favorite station to try to soothe the moment. After a couple songs, Jesse's young mind forgot about the sadness, and the rest of the ride consisted of various head bops and dance breaks.

Jesse ran into the house and started taking all the pieces out of the toy foam gun box and setting everything up to battle with the army men he was also gifted. Mark grabbed a bottle of water out of the fridge and leaned on the island to drink it, watching his elated son have the day of his life. Holly nudged his arm slightly to get his attention.

"Do you think it's weird? Leslie being this isolated, away from the family?" she asked out of curiosity.

"Honestly, I know she drove me absolutely crazy, but it's definitely out of character for her to not talk to her family like this. I mean, not staying at the hospital to see Lizzie when she was awake?" he replied. He walked into the master bedroom and texted Leslie to see if she would answer. Five minutes later, he changed his mind, and mentally prepared as he dialed the number.

"Hello?" an exhausted but familiar voice answered.

"Leslie, is that you?" Mark asked in shock.

"Ya? What?" she replied.

"You do know it's Jesse's birthday, right?" he asked.

"Oh, that is today," Leslie answered with a tired, surprised voice.

"You really should talk to him," Mark suggested.

"I heard his message. Tell him I love him," Leslie replied.

"It will mean more coming from you. He's worried about you. Frankly, everyone is worried about you. You've been really isolated from everyone, and it's out of character for you," Mark explained, trying to convey his concern.

"My character, huh? You know so much about my character," she started.

"That's not fair and you know it," Mark interrupted.

"It doesn't matter. I'm fine. The kid is the one who has issues. Kid wakes up screaming half of the time, just like his sister did," she confessed.

"Just promise me you'll keep in contact with your kids. I don't care if I don't hear from you, but you still have kids that need you in their lives. And that "kid" you talk of is your son." Before he could say more or ask what she meant, he heard a click and a ring as Leslie hung up the phone. Mark looked up to see Holly in the doorway.

"That good, huh?" she asked.

"About as good as it's gonna get," Mark answered. "She said something about him waking up screaming. I just don't know." They both walked out of the bedroom to see the Battle of the Brown-Headed Boy in full pursuit, Jesse shooting down any soldier who got in the way of the TV remote. Mark and Holly watched until the end of the battle, when Jesse thrust his arms in the air celebrating his victory.

"Jesse, why don't you set up another battle, and I'll show you some tricks," Mark suggested. Jesse's eyes lit up like stars and hurried to set the army men back up. Mark slowly pulled another toy foam gun out of the box and filled it with Styrofoam bullets. Suddenly, Jesse felt a slight press on the back of his head. He swung his body to look behind him, only to see his flesh and blood betraying his parental oath. Jesse quickly grabbed his toy foam gun to shoot back. Mark ducked behind couches and chairs to avoid the bullets as he and Jesse shot at each other back and forth. Mark ran out of bullets, and before he could reload, was tackled to the ground by his young son. Rolling around and wrestling on the floor, Mark was two counts away from declaring victory before a piece of Styrofoam slapped him right between the eyes. The boys both stopped what they are doing and looked up to see Holly with both toy foam guns locked, loaded, and ready to go. They jumped up and ran screaming through the house as Holly pelted them with bullets. She cornered both of them in the kitchen, and as they begged for mercy, she proclaimed, "Ha! Girls can do it better." Mark started to chuckle and shake his head, while Jesse stuck out his tongue and walked away, telling her the war wasn't over.

PROTEST

LIZZIE

It felt like years that I had been in this hospital. I was sure it had only been like two to two and a half months, but being stuck in the same stupid bed for so long made time go by like snails trying to move through molasses…. And I was not even sure I knew what molasses was. I just heard people a lot older than me talking about it. The school had been all over the news at the time because they really had not started any of the construction on the repairs yet, and people were getting more and more frustrated. The nurse announced there was a huge story on it that would be on the news later today, so it looked like we were going to have a much needed but depressing break from game show reruns.

"Hey doc, I'm curious. What is the plan with treatments now? Will I be able to start more physical therapy yet? I've been doing really well with what we've been doing, and I'm ready for more," I asked when I saw his white coat floating above the ground.

"Not yet. It looks like your body is rejecting some of the grafts, especially around your core and your back. We will need to get those healed up before we have you enrolled in any kind of strenuous physical therapy. Until then, we'll stick with the absolute basics," he replied. I felt my face droop, and my shoulders stiffened. This was the goal for weeks. I looked out the window, dreaming of the day when I could finally take care of myself again, but it was starting to get more and more hopeless. I was still borderline screeching in pain every time I moved, but I needed something. I really was doing well. What gives?

"Ugggghhhhhh, I just want to get out of this bed," I announced, tossing a towel in his direction. My arms folded, and my lips pursed to the side of my cheek, trying to hide the pain of folding them. I bit my tongue to try to keep from saying something unpleasant or unladylike.

"I know, but we need your body to focus on healing the skin right now," he replied before I could continue complaining. My eyes rolled as he exited the room. The nurses came in to help me roll to my side and told me he was on one that day. I chuckled a little bit at the joke as they smirked. It was nice to have confidants that I could joke around with while I was there.

"Is he sure there is nothing else they can do? Is he serious that this just takes time?" I asked. Lyla nodded her head and looked away, not able to say anything to comfort me. "Why does everything take so much time?"

Lyla woke me up from my afternoon nap to let me know the news was on. She turned on the TV, switching the channel over. The screen was filled with angry parents holding signs about protecting the kids and supporting the teachers. Mr. Davidson walked through the crowd up to the podium and started pointing to reporters to answer questions.

"This small town got that much attention?" I asked. Nothing happened there. It was so small, people usually jumped to look out the window at the mere sound of a siren.

"Apparently, they said there were reporters from states away. It's possible it might catch national attention soon," she replied. My eyes widened as we continued to watch.

"Do you feel responsible for the teen who is currently in the hospital due to her actions saving students from the falling power pole?" one reporter asked.

"I am aware of the heroic story of a girl who pushed students out of the way and took the brunt of the pole's failing. However, it was the choice of this student that caused her injuries, not that of the school," Mr. Davidson explained. I had to bite my tongue. Lyla's eyes widened, and her jaw hit the floor. One parent jumped from the crowd and grabbed a reporter's microphone.

"If that young woman did not jump in the way, my child, as well as multiple others, would be dead. That being said, neglect of the building would have caused pain and tragedy either way. You still believe that is not your responsibility?" she asked. Mr. Davidson ignored that comment and went to other reporters' questions. The crowd of angry parents got louder and louder until it was almost no longer possible to hear the rest of the press conference.

"He is not going to last that much longer," I commented. "Those parents are going to eat him alive."

"He's going to have to go into hiding after this. Did you see him just ignore that mother?" Lyla joked. I nodded my head and mumbled under my breath. Lyla asked what I said, and I just bit my lips and replied with a demure smile to tell her, "Nothing!" The camera shot cut to a reporter in the crowd of parents, and he was explaining a lot of the concerns of the parents regarding their kids. He also brought up many of the teachers' concerns about teaching remotely and having to figure it out themselves. That was when I saw a familiar face in the distance.

"Wait, is that Mom?" I tried to sit up to see better but was brutally reminded that the skin grafts were not holding, throwing me back onto the bed in incredible burning pain. Lyla walked up to the TV, squinting at the screen. She cocked her head to the side and stared at the familiar figure standing in the crowd.

"I.... I think that is your mom," she answered in surprise. We sat in disbelief, seeing that she was present. No one had heard from her in days. Her hair was disheveled, and she wore a dingy brown suit coat, watching the protest around her become more and more volatile. She looked like she was entranced, staring off into the distance and reacting to nothing around her. My brows furrowed, and both Lyla and I sat with our heads cocked to the side in disbelief.

"I want to take some time to speak to the mother of the brave teen that jumped in to save students from utmost tragedy. Leslie, would you like to tell your story?" He turned to her and handed her the mic. She was a pro when in front of the camera;

but this time, she froze in place. Mom's eyes enlarged and her body stiffened. She adjusted her coat and ran her fingers through her hair. I could see her starting to breathe heavier, her hands shaking mildly. I had never known my mom to have stage freight, but something about this was different. Mom cleared her throat and started to speak; the background was filled with angry chants from fellow protesters.

"My daughter, I believe, is being used as a political pawn in a game for the superintendent to avoid responsibility for his neglect on essential repairs that were required for this elementary school. These repairs have been needed for years, and members of the community have continued to voice their concerns, yet to no avail. It should not have to come to the death or dismemberment of a student, teacher, or other community member to bring this case to attention, yet this is what it has come to," she started, her eyes piercing directly to the camera. "My daughter still sits in her hospital bed unable to walk, and her movement overall is extremely limited due to the severity of the burns and injuries to her body. I, and additional support from the community, will be filing suit against the school district for the immediate removal of Superintendent Davidson from his position; we will also be filing charges for neglect and injury to a child. We are also planning to petition the state for additional funds to get this building repaired and getting teachers the appropriate tools to teach their kids, in the meantime, until school can properly resume. The fact that the superintendent is not completing his responsibility of fighting for the school, leaving that responsibility in the hands of those in the community, is absolutely despicable," she ended. Cheers erupted in the background over her speech, and other parents jumped into frame to hug and congratulate Mom. The now wide-eyed Lyla turned to me to see my jaw also to the floor in shock. We stood there in silence as the TV ended the news segment, processing what just happened.

"Wwwww…. woooooow," was all I could muster. "What just happened?"

"I…. I think we can assume your mom is okay?" Lyla commented. I nodded my head, as she slowly exited the room. Silence echoed through the room while I reflected on what I just witnessed. After not hearing from my mom in weeks, to then learn that she was going on this campaign to essentially destroy the school was a case of mental whiplash so bad I could barely see straight. I didn't understand where that announcement came from. I couldn't fathom my prim and proper mother showing up to a massive gathering of people looking as if she was sleeping on the streets for the past few weeks. I didn't like how things were changing. Who was she?

Sophie stormed in a while later, asking if I had seen what just happened on the news. We talked about how surprised we both were to see her in the audience, let alone her appearance and the comments she made. Sophie mentioned how relieved she felt that she finally had a sight of the matriarch that evaded her every contact for the last few weeks. I brought her up to date on what they were planning with treatments and physical therapy, and then we went on about Jesse's birthday party. As bad as I felt missing my kid brother's big birthday party, I was glad it had gone well.

"Have you been over to visit Grandma lately?" I asked.

"Just that one time. I know I need to get back over there but being a mom to three kids brings a lot of challenges. Have you been able to video chat with her more than that one time?" she questioned. I nodded my head. Lyla and her friend had tried to get us together every couple weeks, but it had been a while since our last contact. It had become harder for the nurses to coordinate schedules in order to do so. Life of a nurse, right? Lyla came in a few minutes into the conversation to roll me over, and Sophie asked to show her how things are done so she could help when she was visiting. They rolled me over onto my side while I bit down on the corner of an extra towel, and Lyla showed Sophie how to care for the fresh scars and dying skin grafts on my back. I heard Sophie dry heave behind me when they started to clean one of the wounds. I chuckled a bit hearing her pain, but from the sounds of it, the wound was borderline infected at that point. Lyla called the doctor in to check out the wound, and after an adjustment to the antibiotics, they re-wrapped everything, and I was ordered to stay on my side until everything relaxed. Unfortunately, I was turned away from the chairs and the TV, so Sophie had to maneuver one of the heavy wooden stools around the IV rack and all the machines so we could at least see each other for the time being. Sophie asked how I was doing being out of school for so long. I expressed concern that I couldn't remember anything from my classes, and there was no way I was going to be able to graduate. I felt my voice start to hasten and crack as I explained how I felt.

"I think…… you can do it. If I remember correctly, spring was kind of lax and easy. Although, I didn't take as many AP courses as you have on your plate, so I guess maybe it's not that accurate of a comparison," she said, putting her head in her hand. I just sat and laughed, thanking her for the laugh and the confidence boost. I asked her to remind me what she had her senior year.

"I had AP Chem and AP English all year, and I took the test for AP History before I graduated," she responded. "You were taking the actual AP History class and had AP Calculus and AP Geography too, right?" She asked me. I nodded my head and pursed my lips, not excited about the reminder of how far behind I was.

"Lizzie, is there anything I can do to help you?" Sophie questioned curiously, holding my hand. We sat there in silence as I thought about how to answer her. I really didn't know how to answer. I contemplated for what seemed like forever, but was probably a minute. There wasn't much she could help with right now.

"Sophie, I just want you to live life. Do crazy things with Chris and the kids. Then, come back and tell me all the stories. I want to hear stories. I want to live through you while I'm helpless and stuck here. I need to live life through you."

LESLIE

Leslie watched the crowd of angry parents screaming over the sound of the man at the podium. She squeezed tears out of her eyes as she tried to pull herself together amid the chaos of the protest. She looked at her phone to check the time, seeing a photo of Lizzie and Jesse on her screen, and then she put it back in her pocket. She saw a reporter wandering through with a camera operator talking with various people in the crowd. She turned away from the camera and started walking away to avoid him when a random community member recognized her.

"Hey, it's the mom of that girl!" she heard someone scream. Her heart started beating out of her chest as she heard footsteps running behind her. She tried to make her way through the crowd, only to be met by a blockade of human bodies all equally excited to make her acquaintance. Her hands got clammy as she turned to see a young, enthusiastic kid with a microphone six inches from her face. A hand also waved from behind the camera.

"Will you do an interview with us, please?" the ambitious reporter asked while jumping in place. Leslie said yes without thinking, and suddenly, questions started flying at her from all directions. She started answering out of habit. Disassociation clouded her mind, and she subconsciously co-operated with the reporter, without knowing what she said. When she came back to reality, complete strangers clapping for her, looking at her, hugging her. She tried to call for the reporter as he walked away, but he never heard her calls. One of the angry mothers came up to her and told her how inspirational she was in what she was planning to do.

"Can I ask you something?" Leslie asked, looking around at the crowd staring back at her. "What did I say?" Her face started to go white as time went by, and this mom realized Leslie was serious.

"Wait, do you really not remember?" she asked. Leslie shook her head slowly, scared of what the response would be. The mom repeated everything Leslie said she was doing in the interview. Leslie's eyes protruded out of their places, and her blood rushed to her feet. In no way did she plan for any of this to happen.

"Whatever help you need, you have my full support! You are incredible!" the mom said. Three or four more parents around her agreed, and the mom started gathering everyone's information.

"Wait. Wait. Wait," Leslie said, grabbing the mother's arm. "I can't do this. That wasn't me that was talking. I can't do all this." The parents around her started chanting her name, and the mother nodded her head, telling Leslie that they can do it as a team. The more they cheered, the more she was encouraged, the blood came back to Leslie's face. Her hands stopped tingling, and her breath slowed. She looked to the eager mom. "What is your name?"

"I'm Emily. My husband Daniel and I moved into the school district a couple months ago. I was going to start teaching here next school year," she explained.

"Emily, thank you," Leslie uttered, and then she walked away in shock over the events of the last hour or so. The excited parents watched in confusion as their proposed leader simply left but continued gathering information from everyone around them.

Leslie walked the dreary distance back to her car, sinking into her seat in despair. Her hands started shaking again as she realized the work she was going to have to do. They had it on camera. People knew she was a newscaster. If there was ever a case to hold someone accountable, it was her. The thought soon took over, and she fell apart in the driver's seat, trying to figure out what needed to happen. Everything that happened at the protest was a blur. Her memory was blank. Blood rushed from her face. She wasn't ready to be in public. Now, she just made herself the face of a movement that she herself wasn't sure was able to be moved.

A week later, Leslie received a call from an unknown number. Three rings went by before Leslie decided to answer the phone instead of sending it to voicemail.

"Leslie?" a familiar, but unrecognized voice asked.

"Yaaa? ... Who is this?" Leslie replied.

"This is Emily… from the protest?" Emily curiously answered. Leslie now remembered the happy mom from the protest.

"Ohhhh… Hi! How did you get my number?" Leslie probed.

"Uhmmm you're a newscaster, so I called your work and asked about you, and they gave me your number right away. Apparently, they're really excited about what you are doing as well," Emily explained. Leslie's heart dropped to her stomach, and her stomach dropped to her feet.

"Look, Emily, I don't think we can…" she started.

"We have 500 signatures so far," Emily interrupted.

"Wait… what?" Leslie asked.

"The other parents and I have gotten 500 signatures for the state so far. Everyone is working so hard, and it's creating a lot of buzz. People want to help. And guess what? One of the parents is a lawyer and is offering to take the case pro bono!" Emily disclosed. Leslie dropped to her couch and put her hand over her mouth.

"What? I didn't think this was real. I didn't even think about a lawyer. I didn't even think my words would have this much impact," Leslie stated. "Why are you doing all this, Emily?"

"I saw how you held yourself. You meant every word you said, even if you didn't remember exactly what you said. It inspired me, Leslie. It inspired all of us. We want to be a part of that change. I know I'm still new to the area, but I've already heard absolute horror stories about Mr. Davidson. We need him to go, and you can be the wrecking ball to do it," she encouraged. Leslie smiled, realizing she had such comfort in someone who was practically a stranger.

"Emily, I must confess something. I'm still in a very vulnerable state right now. It's been a while since I've had contact with my family, and my daughter is still in the hospital. Life is still a lot, so I need your help. And a lot of it," Leslie explained. Emily cheerfully agreed to do anything needed to support Leslie and mentioned she would send contact information for other people in the group and would send Leslie anything else she needed. Leslie thanked her and they hung up the phones. "I'm really going to do this? Am I going to do this? Why am I doing this? Oh God… This is happening." She mumbled to herself. She put her head in her hands and froze. Finding it hard to breathe, she sat thinking about the roller coaster she was about to be strapped into.

Leslie tossed and turned all night thinking about what the next few months would look like. Sleep seemed so far away from her. She got out of bed the next morning and brewed a cup of coffee, only to turn around and realize that she had let the house go. She cringed at the state the kitchen had become: empty pizza boxes, empty tubs of leftovers stacked on the counters, and sticky spaces where old soda cans and icing had been left for weeks. She took the coffee mug and walked back into her bedroom for some peace. She thought long and hard about her next steps while she drank the coffee, asking herself if this was something she really wanted or needed to do.

She thought about Lizzie, and how much pain she last saw her in. She needed to do this. She took the last sip of her cup, took a deep breath, and walked back out to the kitchen. She dug the roll of trash bags out of the drawer and emptied the countertops of the hoard of trash and waste that had accumulated over the past couple weeks. She slid the melted ice cream tubs into the trash, and she dry-heaved while washing the molding dishes, but it was soon enough that her house started to look more like a house instead of an endless pit of despair.

DELICATE

LIZZIE

I was pushing on being stuck in that hospital bed for about three months. My body finally decided to stop rejecting the skin grafts and was slowly healing from the constant trauma from the accident and subsequent infections. I cringed at the scars that had formed from the dead tissue and repeated graft removals, a map of struggle and pain that I will never be able to forget. Physical therapy continued to be very gentle and basic, as to not irritate the scars, but I was so bored. It had been a couple weeks since Sophie came, and I still hadn't seen Mom around. Lyla went on vacation with her family, and her replacement was an absolute disaster. When I wasn't being tossed around like a rag doll getting flipped, or pain medication showing up long after I initially needed it, I had been completely alone for some time.

I finally had to ask to have the television turned off for the time being because I was so done with endless TV game show reruns, I could have thrown up. Since the grafts were taking, it seemed the raw, new layers of skin were intensely sensitive, and I had been calling for pain medication more than I usually would have. I started biting actual holes in the towel I stuffed in my mouth to muffle screams when they came in to roll me over.

I could move my lower arm just enough to reach my hand to my face to wipe away the tears that I had been crying being here so alone. I hadn't been able to connect with Grandma for a few weeks. Everything just felt empty and alone. I just wanted to see my family, be with my family. I was so sick of this madness...

"I'mmmm baaaackk," Lyla announced as she walked into my room a couple days later. I nearly jumped out of bed hearing her familiar voice, but the excitement stretched my still growing-back skin to the point I flopped back into my bed in searing pain, reminding me once again that I was not getting out of that bed anytime soon. I screamed with excitement to have my friend back. I made her tell me all about her vacation while she jumped to the IV stand to check on the numbers. She was not walking out of that room without telling me everything.

I got to hear about her trip to the coast; the trip filled with ocean swims and boat rides, whale watching and deep-sea fishing. Her shopping trips to random hole-in-the-wall shops and eating from the endless street tacos and food trucks along the boardwalk. She recounted the cuddle-filled evenings with her children, laying in the sun all day, and the much-needed time with her family. She talked about all the many game nights she was able to have with her kids, winning the family poker tournament, the date night with her wife that ended up with them being sprayed with water from cars hitting the puddle too hard, and the joys of exploring the city around her. The only thing I wanted to hear about was being near the ocean. I dreamt of walking in the sand, swimming in the waves, feeling free. Lyla got so excited talking about the ocean, and then she said she remembered something in her bag.

"Hey, yo, I actually got something for you," she mentioned as she reached into her bag. Curiosity overwhelmed me as I tried to sit myself up as much as I could without throwing myself into another painful blaze of fiery madness. She pulled a mason jar out of her bag, and it was filled with sand from the beach. She gently set the jar in my lap, and my eyes grew wide with excitement. I reached down and held the jar in my hands, tipping it back and forth and watching the sand fall to the other side of the jar.

"Really?" I looked into her face. "You got this for me? Why?" Tears started to slowly well up in my tear ducts. I never expected her be so kind to me. She ran her fingers through my hair and held my hand.

"I know how much you want to get out of this bed. I know how much you miss being able to walk and do things for yourself. So…. I brought some of the beach to you," she declared. I couldn't help but smile while my heart melted seeing this much kindness and concern from someone whose job was to take care of me. She didn't have to do this. She opened the jar, and I held it to my face so I could smell the ocean in my hands. I carefully let one finger drop into the jar and stir around in the sand. The doctor came in and saw me playing with sand, practically having a heart attack.

"No, no, no, no, no, no…. You cannot be exposing yourself to this," he said as he took the jar from Lyla's hand. He was about to dump it in the trash before she jumped in.

"Stop! It's mine! Do not dump that!" she yelled as she grabbed the jar and quickly put the lid back on.

"I expected better from you. You know she can't expose herself to anything external that could put her at risk for infection," Doctor James explained.

"She's in a fucking hospital. She's been exposed to far worse. But she's healing. She's fine," Lyla barked. She stood between the doctor and my bed, her hands sitting sternly on her hips.

"STOP!" I screamed. "It was my choice. Be pissed at me. The skin on my fingers is fine. One wipe of an anti-bacterial and good to go." I looked over to Lyla briefly, who got what I was saying and grabbed a wipe.

"Whatever. You need to be more careful," the doctor firmly warned. "How are you feeling today?"

"Fine, until you walked in just now."

"I meant your skin… ma'am," Doctor James reiterated.

"Back is still in searing pain, soooooo…. Same as it was last time you checked," I explained as I rolled my eyes.

"I can see I'm getting nowhere right now. I'm going to check on the other patients," he said. He started to open the door to leave the room.

"Wait, I have a question," I interrupted. "Can I start more physical therapy yet? I've literally been asking for weeks. The basics aren't enough anymore."

"You are not ready," the doctor simply answered.

"Come on, something dude. I need to get out of this bed," I mentioned.

"You are not ready," he repeated.

"Yes, I am!" I argued back.

"What if…" Lyla jumped in. "What if I got a couple more nurses and we at least were able to sit her in a wheelchair and then back in the bed? Something quick and safe, and she wouldn't need to do anything strenuous herself?" she asked hesitantly.

"You know what? Since you've obviously turned my staff against me, do what you want. You better not give yourself an infection," he pointed at me as he stomped out of the room. I looked at Lyla, who rolled her eyes and put her head in her hand.

"Good God, what's up with him today?" she asked.

"No idea. He's been a little short all week," I explained. "But yo, were you serious about that chair thing?" I asked hopefully, as my eyes started to twinkle.

"A little bit. Are you sure you want to do that?" she asked. "I saw you when I first came in. You are still in a LOT of pain," she explained.

"I have been in this pathetic bed for almost 3 months at this point. It's worth it," I proclaimed. She let me know it might be a little bit, but she would get everything planned and get things taken care of. I whispered "yes" under my breath as she walked out of the room. "I can get out of this bed! It's about time!" I screamed to myself. My jaws cramped in excitement as I couldn't stop smiling and thinking about what it would be like to finally get out of here.

Later that afternoon, Lyla came back and announced she had talked to a couple other nurses and the physical therapist who were willing to come help with our request. I smiled and sat myself up as much as I could as she dragged in a wheelchair, and a variety of towels and clothes. She walked up to the side of my bed to speak with me. She was a little nervous.

"Are you sure you want to do this? It's going to be painful," she started. "It will probably be the most painful thing you've ever done, Lizzie. I mean it. You need to be 100% sure."

"However painful it's going to be, that is how sure I am," I proclaimed I was ready to do this, at any cost. The other nurses started to walk in and straighten everything up so there was a clear path to the wheelchair and back. My instruction was not to move. They were going to wrap me in the blanket underneath me and pick me up in that, so they didn't touch my bare skin. I motioned for a towel to put in my mouth before they counted to three. I felt a couple of strong, muscle-laden arms slide under my back and under my legs, searing the delicate layers of skin. I squealed in pain as I felt the pressure of them removing me from the bed. Lyla anxiously told everyone to stop, and she asked me again if I was ready to do this. I nodded my head with burning tears in my eyes. We came this far. In my mind, it was too late to turn back.

Searing pain like 1,000 knives slid across my skin as they lifted me from the bed and carried me to the chair. The weight of my body now sitting on my legs felt like I was being thrown into a bonfire. I screamed into the towel as they picked me up again and carried me to the bed. After putting me down, I heard the other nurses apologizing while another placed morphine into my IV. The pressure and stress of being removed from the bed seared into my brain, the pain of the burns throwing me back to the accident; my mind flashed back to the flames enveloping my body, the weight of the pole snapping my back, and feeling my skin crumble away at the paramedics' every touch. Inconsolable tears left my eyes as I tried to comprehend the ensuing events and struggled to differentiate the past from the reality of the present. Lyla started to cry tears of guilt as she wiped away tears from my face and running her fingers through my hair. She continued to tell me "I'm sorry" over and over as I flinched in pain with all my nerves firing at once. She walked over to close the door as she saw people starting to look into the room to see what was going on. She caught a glimpse of Doctor James shaking his head before she came back over to comfort me. I continued to sob for what seemed like hours before my body slowly fell asleep.

MARK

Mark had just driven the car into the driveway from bringing Jesse home from school when Holly walked out the door to take the trash outside. They met each other at the entrance of their humble abode when Jesse started talking excitedly about what he did in school that day. After he went on and on talking about volcanoes and dinosaurs and the 100% on his spelling test, Jesse plopped on the couch and sighed, remembering the epic day he had. Mark grabbed a water from the fridge and sat next to him on the couch and reclined the seat.

"So, kid… We haven't had one call this week about fights in school, which means we should celebrate. What do you want to do this weekend?" he asked his excited son.

"I don't know. We already went bowling. I don't want to go skating again," he replied as he showed his dad the still-healing scrape on his elbow. "Can we stay home and play videogames?"

"If that is what you would like to do, we can do that," Mark smiled. The boys relaxed, sprawled out on the couch with the TV on the sports channel for the newest golf tournament. Holly put freshly baked chocolate chip cookies on the cooling rack and walked into the room to find them fast asleep; Jesse was wrapped around Mark's arm, and Mark had drool falling down his face. She chuckled at the sight, walking to the kitchen where she continued to put dinner together. She turned the stove on to boil the pot of water she previously filled and pulled out the leftover grilled chicken and chopped it up. After slicing up the rest of the vegetables and throwing them into the boiling water, she snuck into the living room to check on her sleeping "children."

Both still fast asleep, Holly thought of an idea that she decided was perfect for this moment. She stumbled her way over Jesse's backpack and stack of toys to her purse that was sitting by the front door. She dug through the bag and found her bright red lipstick and her eyeliner; she walked back over the stack of toys and undid the lids of the makeup, carefully outlining the boys' lips and eyebrows in funny shapes. She froze every time the boys seemingly felt a disturbance in their presence but sighed when they never woke up. She finished her living art pieces and raced back into the kitchen to hide the evidence and drain the noodles that had been cooking in the meantime. She continued on her merry way, pretending nothing ever happened.

About half an hour later, she heard rustling coming from the couch. Mark had stretched his arms into the air and swiped his hand across his face, smearing the makeup all over his arm. His eyes half closed, he laid his arms on the couch and continued to relax. Holly held her tongue, trying her hardest not to burst out laughing from what she just witnessed. She pulled the chicken alfredo out of the oven and set it on the counter to cool a little bit, and then she walked over to the couch to wake everyone up.

"Are you boys ready for dinner?" she asked sweetly as she gently shook Jesse awake.

"What time is it?" he asked with a huge yawn.

"Time for dinner. Y'all wanna get washed up?" Holly suggested. Jesse looked over to Mark, and his eyes widened with what he saw. Holly couldn't help but chuckle, which was noticed by Mark.

"What was that?" Mark asked suspiciously.

"What?" she replied, trying to act confused.

"You laughed. I saw it. What did you do?" he asked as he lifted his arm to his forehead. He noticed the bright red streaks across his hand, and he looked over to see a bold, angry emoji face on his son. "You didn't?" he asked, whipping his head back around to look at Holly. She simply stood behind the couch with her arms crossed and an evil grin on her face. She put her hand over her mouth as she broke out in chuckles and walked away to grab dishes to set the table.

"Boy, you may wanna go look in the mirror," he said to a still wide-eyed Jesse. Jesse jumped from the couch and ran to the bathroom.

"Noooooo! Ew ew ew!" he shouted in the distance, grabbing the towel on the sink and scraping the makeup off his face. "You're gross!" As he smeared the red lipstick all over his face, Holly marched in, grabbed the makeup wipes, and started showing Jesse how to properly wipe the makeup off his face. He glared at her the entire time, planning his impending revenge as he tried to push her away. Mark snatched a few makeup wipes and started cleaning off his own face and arm. They all walked back out, and Holly started serving dinner to the boys, who were now sitting at the dining room table.

She continued to chuckle at her much successful prank, while the boys glared at her in suspicion. Moments of silence ensued as they all started their meal; then Jesse stopped and put his fork down. Everyone else at the table stopped and raised their heads to look at him. Jesse cleared his throat.

"Dad, can I see Lizzie?" he asked quietly. Holly and Mark just looked at Jesse, bewildered that his sister was suddenly on his mind.

"What?" Holly asked.

"I want to go see Lizzie. I miss her. I haven't been able to see her since she left," he replied, looking down at his dinner.

"Uhmmmm," Holly started. She looked at Mark. "I can probably take you in a couple days," she proposed.

"Wait…." Mark interrupted. "Maybe I should take you," he said. "I haven't been up there to see her either." Holly whipped her head around to look at Mark, her eyes wider than her face. Everyone looked around at each other in silence, confusion seen on their faces.

"Why…. don't…. we all go?" Holly asked hesitantly. Mark timidly smiled at her, and Jesse nodded his head excitedly. They continued eating their dinner, and Jesse talked enthusiastically about when he wanted to go to the hospital until he lost attention and decided that videogames were next on the evening's agenda. After asking to be excused, Jesse raced to the consoles and grabbed the controllers as if Lizzie's name hadn't come up at all that day.

SOPHIE

"Hello?" Sophie answered as the picked up the phone.

"Hi Sophie, it's Dad," Mark responded.

"Hi Dad. It's good to hear from you. Is everything okay? It's not often that you call me," she questioned.

"Everything is good, don't worry. Uhmmm… I wanted to talk to you about something… someone… about Holly," he initiated. Sophie was caught off guard. She paused folding laundry and sat down on her bed.

"What about her? You guys are okay, right?" she continued to question.

"Ya, we're still fine. Uhmmm… what I wanted to ask is…. what do you truly think and feel about her?" he asked hesitantly, his nerves pulsing from all the possible answers to that question.

"Uhmmm…. okay…. strange question… but I really like her. You two look like you really enjoy each other, and she's really kind to the rest of the family. Why are you asking me?"

"The reason I am asking… is that I've been thinking about it for a while… of asking her to marry me," he confessed.

"Really? You totally should!" Sophie asked excitedly. "That's so great, Dad! I'm so excited for you guys!"

"Thank you. I really do love her, Sophie. I really think she's the one this time." Sophie smiled as Mark went on about his dream girl. "We are going to take Jesse to see Lizzie in a couple days, and I think I want to propose in the hospital, with everyone there. Would you mind coming down?" he asked.

"Dad, I wouldn't miss it for the world! I will be there. I love you, Dad," she exclaimed, smiling from ear to ear. She couldn't wait to tell Chris and the kids. They all loved Holly to death. It was then, that she finally felt her family was starting to piece itself   back   together.

MY BABIES

LESLIE

Leslie stood in front of her full-length mirror, adjusting her suit and getting ready for the meeting with Emily and the lawyer. She wiped drops of sweat from her forehead, reminding herself to breathe through the nervous tremors. It had been hours of phone calls and letters to garner more signatures to send to the state with the petition; Leslie was starting to get a little excited about the impact she could possibly make. She picked up her ringing phone and noticed it was Emily.

"Hey girl! Are you ready? I'm outside!" Emily blurted out.

"I'm on my way," Leslie responded as she hung up the phone. She grabbed her tote bag and stumbled down the stairs as she tried to keep her feet underneath her. She hopped into the passenger seat of Emily's car, and they made their way the 120 miles to the lawyer's office.

"How many signatures are we at now?" Leslie asked curiously.

"We got together last week and compiled the lists. There were some people that even went to nearby cities and gathered signatures. We have 12,433 signatures to start the petition!" Emily squeaked excitedly. Leslie's eyes widened after hearing that number. They relished in the seemingly early success of their petition as they drove up to the lawyer's office. The sound of clacking high heels echoed through the entryway as Emily and Leslie looked around to find the right room. Emily pointed the way, and Leslie followed as they met the lawyer at the door of his office.

"Hello, Matt!" Emily nearly shouted in excitement as she wrapped her arms around him. He awkwardly received the hug and smiled. He noticed Leslie in the background and nodded his head; he tried to push away from Emily kindly as he worked his way over to shake Leslie's hand.

"Hello, ladies. Obviously, we have met," he started while looking at Emily, then turning his gaze back to Leslie. "My name is Matt Walker. I've practiced as an attorney for 13 years. My children have already graduated school in the district, but I still have a soft spot for the community and want to help where I can. I've had my own issues with the superintendent, but I believe in your cause," he continued to explain while almost staring into Leslie's eyes. He directed the ladies into his office so they could continue the conversation.

"So, Leslie, I do recognize you from the local news. I haven't seen you on the screen for a while," he commented.

"I took a leave of absence from work so I could be with my daughter. It came at a right time, I guess, because I've had a lot go on personally, lately as well," she tried to explain as vaguely as she could. She still didn't trust this near complete stranger enough to explain that she hadn't left the house in weeks, other than the appearance at the protest.

"I'm glad your workplace is understanding of the need to make time for your family," Matt replied, looking down at his paperwork and missing Leslie's face wincing. Her boss had been calling her for the past couple days asking when she was going to come back. "Emily, I see you and your group have gathered almost 12,500 signatures. That is very impressive," he commented. Emily nodded in excitement.

"And we are getting more," she squealed.

"That is fantastic. Keep going on those signatures. The more the better. So, due to personal reasons, I have kept documented incidences or 'scandals'" he started explaining, using finger quotes around the word scandals, "having the superintendent as the prime subject. He's been involved not only with neglect of the repairs to the building," he started as he quickly eyed Leslie, making sure his reference to the accident didn't offend her. "He has also been involved in the defense of his secretary that embezzled funds from the district, and his mismanagement of the trust that lost $250,000, which put the district in a budget crisis for a few years, as you probably remember." Leslie nodded her head, remembering the past couple years of crowdfunding and budget cuts that the district needed. "He also didn't properly allocate the funds from the bond that passed five years ago, which triggered an audit of the district's accounts."

Leslie and Emily sat in silence, eyes widened so far that they could at any moment pop out. The information this lawyer had collected on Mr. Davidson, the amount of damage this individual had done was impressive, but even more shocking was the amount of time he had been able to stay in the district in the position he held. Tears started to trickle from Emily's face, as she started to quietly chant to herself, "I almost worked for this man. I could potentially work for this man. I can't work for this man." Leslie placed her hand on Emily's wrist to try to comfort her.

"I'm afraid to ask this, but has there been anything else he has done?" she asked Matt.

"There are rumors that he has made a collection of inappropriate and offensive comments about students, teachers, administrators, etc. Do you ladies know of anyone that has had less-than-pleasant experiences with this man?" he asked. Emily adjusted her posture.

"Uhmmmm," she started, before she started to break down even more. "My nephew. He's had trouble with his grades. We haven't had him tested yet, but plan to. We suspect he might have some learning disabilities that we didn't see early on that are now affecting him. He was in study hall with Mr. Davidson, when this happened. Mr. Davidson knew of his falling grades and difficulties in class, and he said that my nephew wasn't going to amount to anything and that he should just give up now. In front of the rest of the students in the room. Out loud. He publicly humiliated a teenage kid," she struggled to verbalize in between the tears. Matt wiped the sweat from his brow and sat back in his chair in shock.

"Emily, thank you for being brave enough to tell that story. Really, thank you. We need this information. We need more stories like this," he started to preach. "Anything. If you hear any stories of racial slurs, student defamation or bullying, perverted statements, anything," he continued.

"I can talk to the group to see if they have had similar experiences," Leslie spoke up while rubbing Emily's back to comfort her. "Thank you for your story, Emily. That must be hard. No one has the right to ever say that to a child."

"No. A man like that should NOT be in a position to lead a child," Matt agreed. The meeting continued with Matt explaining what the process was going to be like. There would be two different trials due to all the information he had. One would be suing the district for the removal of the superintendent and request for expenses to assist the teachers until the school is repaired. The next trial will be the criminal neglect and potential embezzlement trial for Mr. Davidson himself. Matt explained that the trial could potentially take months, and that the trials, especially the criminal trial, would take place in the state capital, which was another six hours away. Leslie put her head in her hand, trying to think of a way she could be in more than one place at once. There was no way she could return to work, or even take care of things at home while she was taking part in those trials.

"I can take care of everything here, I'm not working until fall, and I don't have any children, so I can also shuttle back and forth when needed," Emily choked out.

"You're willing to do that?" Leslie asked in astonishment. Emily nodded her head and mentioned that her husband Andrew had also been leading the way in gathering signatures in nearby cities, so they had both been travelling a lot.

"Well, it sounds like I need to move?" Leslie asked hesitantly.

"You don't have to move, but I just want you to be aware of what will be involved if this trial proceeds, and I do believe we have enough to ensure that it will," Matt explained. They sat in silent thought for a few moments until Leslie made a decision.

"It's fine. I want to see this through. It's going to be a change that is needed. I'm the only one at home right now, and I honestly don't know if I want to go back to work at the station. Why not?" she started. "I'll need a little bit of time to get things situated and sell my house, but let's make sure this man pays for what he has done.... Or hasn't done in some cases," she stated. Matt nodded his head in agreeance, as did Emily, while blowing her nose in the background.

"If that is what you want to do, I will help wherever I can," Matt explained. "I have a couple properties near the capital, so you are more than welcome to set up headquarters in one of them. Let me know if you need anything for your daughter as well," he slipped in. Leslie blinked a couple times in surprise at the comment, and then thanked him for the support. The meeting adjourned shortly after with Matt handing Leslie his contact information and walking them out of the building. He held the door open as Leslie wrapped her arm around a still emotional Emily. Matt winked at Leslie as they walked away from each other's presence. Leslie offered to drive home, which Emily gladly agreed to, and they settled themselves into the car. Leslie took Matt's card he had given her and put it in the center console, not before seeing a note from him saying to "call him." She didn't say anything to Emily, and they drove home in silence, as Emily had essentially cried herself to sleep. "Call me? He also winked at me. Hmm."

SOPHIE

Sophie drove the long drive to the hospital in silence. Excited, nervous, happy silence. The thought of seeing her bachelor father re-marry someone that the whole family appreciated excited her. She told her children the news after she got the announcement, and they jumped up and down, screaming with overwhelming child joy that their pop-pop was getting married. She thought back to telling them the news, remembering them running down the hallway of the house throwing stuffed animals and costume jewelry in the air in excitement. She thought about that memory for the entire drive and couldn't stop smiling as she passed countless delivery vans and semi-trucks on the freeway. This was also the first time that her father and little brother were going to see Lizzie, so the thought of seeing them re-unite melted her heart as she continued to drive. She took a deep breath and looked towards her husband, Chris, in the passenger seat. He grabbed her hand and nodded his smiling head with encouragement as they continued their journey to the hospital.

JESSIE

Jesse ran up and down the hallway of the house asking Mark and Holly what he needed to bring to the hospital.

"Can I bring a present? Do you think she would like my trucks? What should I bring? How should I do my hair? What do I wear? What do you wear to hospitals?" he asked over and over as they packed up a day bag with snacks and drinks for the road trip to the hospital. Holly chuckled as Mark kept rolling his eyes and looking to the ceiling, flabbergasted at the number of questions this hyperactive third grader could ask. He shuffled the tablet to Jesse to go play for a minute while they finished getting things ready. Mark made a quick call to Sophie to make sure she was still coming and checked his laptop for any unread messages.

"You about ready?" Holly asked as she walked in on Mark shutting down his laptop. Mark nodded his head and called for Jesse to grab a jacket and put on his shoes. Jesse shook with excitement to the point he struggled as he put his shoes on the wrong feet and put his jacket on inside-out, but he didn't care. He was about to go on another adventure, and it had been months since he had seen his big sister.

"Now Jesse," Holly said as she knelt to his side. "We must warn you; Lizzie looks very different now, okay? We just want to try to prepare you for what you might see," she continued to explain. Jesse looked at her confused.

"Different? How? She still looks like Lizzie though, right?" he asked, bewildered.

"Yes, Jesse, she does still look like Lizzie, but she does have a lot of scars on her face, and she might not be able to move very well. As much as she looks like Lizzie, she still looks very different," she tried to explain before Mark interrupted.

"Okay, let's head to the car," he announced, giving Holly a stern look straight into the eyes to say that was enough. She stood back up and grabbed the jacket laid on Mark's arm, and they all departed from the house and loaded up the car. Jesse jumped into the car while Mark and Holly put the bags in the trunk. After closing the door, Mark laid his hand on Holly's shoulder.

"Holly, can we not freak out the kid? You're almost making this out to sound like Lizzie is the monster in the closet or something," he asked.

"Mark, he's not going to recognize her. I just want him to be aware that things are going to be different. And perhaps you need to be aware, too," she explained. Mark shook his head and groaned as he marched toward the driver's side door. "This might end up being a tougher trip than expected," he mumbled to himself.

"Did you say something, Dad?" Jesse asked excitedly. Mark shook his head, backing the car out of the driveway and sneaking a smile and a wink to his son fidgeting in the back seat.

LESLIE

Leslie paced back and forth through her house trying to find the right words to say when she finally broke the news to her kids that the house got sold, and she was officially moving to the state capital. She had Jesse's belongings all packed up and next to the fireplace in the living room, ready to be picked up. She was still debating what to do with all of Lizzie's things. She hoped that Sophie could take care of them and if anything, she would get a storage unit while Lizzie stayed in the hospital. That would have to be something she figured out when she got to the hospital. Leslie's belongings had already been moved to the new condo provided by the lawyer, Matt, so all she had left to do was say her goodbyes.

She drove the quiet trip to the hospital with the low sound of pop music coming through the stereo, taking deep breaths, and continuing to think about what she wanted to say to her kids. She would start with Lizzie, then stop at Sophie's house on the way, and then call Jesse on her way to her new place. She knew it would be too painful to tell him in person. Plus, it would give Mark less ammunition to say no, if she was already gone. She shook out her hands one-by-one to get rid of the nervous, tingly feeling that had settled in her fingertips. She parked in her usual spot in the hospital parking lot and walked towards the front entrance. After checking in, she made her way down the familiar, dreary hallway to her daughter's hospital room.

"Hi honey," she cheerfully announced as she walked into the room. "Oh, hey Sophie, I didn't know you would be here." Lizzie and Sophie turned to see their mother for the first time in weeks. Their eyebrows furrowed, and their heads tilted to the side in wonder.

"Uhmmm, ya. Sometimes I come and see my little sister," Sophie answered somewhat brazen, disappointed, and frustrated with her mother's absence. "Where have you been?" Lizzie bumped Sophie with her arm lightly to tell her to stop.

"I'm here now, aren't I?" Leslie answered with a cheery smile on her face. She walked up to Lizzie's bed and smiled at her barely conscious daughter. "How are you dear?"

"I'm okay. Just confused. You haven't been here in a long time, so I'm just trying to figure out what is going on," Lizzie explained.

"Maybe I've been here, but you were asleep, so you can't remember," Leslie tried to explain.

"Mom, don't. You know you haven't been

here in weeks," Sophie jumped in. "Everyone here knows you haven't been here in weeks. Don't try to gaslight Lizzie. It's the last thing she needs."

"Mom, I've missed you. Where have you been?" Lizzie spoke up.

"There's been a lot going on at home," Leslie started. "Did you hear we are suing the superintendent?" Sophie and Lizzie nodded. "I've been working on helping get things together for the case against Mr. Davidson. Which…. brings me to what I wanted to talk to you about. And since Sophie is here too, I can tell you both at one time." Leslie started to explain. As she finished her sentence, Holly walked into the room, followed by Jesse and Mark. Sophie stood from her seat, and Lizzie's eyes widened and started to water seeing her little brother and father for the first time since the accident.

"Dad? Jesse?" she mustered through a cloud of tears that quickly enveloped her face. Jesse ran to the side of the bed and froze. He stared at his sister for a long moment, a look of shock sat on his face by how different she really did look.

"Lizzie? That's you? I've missed you!" he almost shouted as he attempted to jump onto the bed to hug his sister. He backed off when Lizzie jumped and squealed in pain. Holly ran to Jesse's side and explained that Lizzie was still healing, and that he needed to be gentle. Lyla ran in to see what the commotion was. She, along with Holly, then explained to Jesse how he could hold his sister's hand lightly without pain, and he held her hand to his face, feeling her touch for the first time in months. Mark stood by the doorway, watching the tender moment between his children take place. Sophie walked around the room and greeted her father with a hug, and mentioned she was glad everyone had made the trip safely. Leslie stood in the middle of the room defeated that her plan wasn't going her way, and she now had to worry about her young son's reaction to the news, as well as her ex-husband.

"So, you finally decided to make it, huh?" she mentioned with her arms folded. Mark continued to hold his arm around Sophie as he walked farther into the room, closer to his girlfriend and young son.

"I needed to be ready, Leslie. You know what that first moment looked like. Just because I haven't been here every moment of every day, doesn't mean that I care any less than you do," Mark replied. The room sat quiet, as the individuals in it realized that Mark had no idea. Sophie pushed away from her father.

"Dad, you didn't know? Mom hasn't been here in weeks," she tried to explain softly. "And when she was here, she always argued with the doctors and she's kind of been terrible to hospital staff." Mark eyed Leslie angrily and shook his head in disbelief because of what he just heard.

"Wait. You haven't been here all along? So, who has been here with our daughter all this time? Has she been alone? Why did no one tell me?" he grilled angrily.

"She's fine. Sophie's been here whenever she can, and she's not a child, Mark," Leslie replied audaciously.

"She is too a child, Leslie. How dare you lead me on to think you've been here the entire time when you've basically abandoned her," he started to argue, until Holly came up to him and started to usher him out of the room. Lizzie's heart monitor started to sound off. Lyla ran in and ushered more people out of the room while she took care of Lizzie.

JESSE

Lyla allowed Jesse to stay by Lizzie's side while she reset the machines and placed some medicine into her IV, only with the understanding that he would be good. Jesse continued to hold Lizzie's hand next to his face, and just stared at his sister, grasping every moment he had with her and making up time for the months that he had missed. Lizzie laid there and watched her little brother feel the moment.

"How are you doing, Buddy?" she asked quietly.

"Good!" he started, excited to hear her voice. "I live with Dad now. He's really fun. We play with toy foam guns a lot, and Holly is really nice."

"That's awesome, Buddy," she smiled. "I'm happy you came up to see me."

"I miss you," he answered sweetly. "You're so happy all the time."

"I try my best," she said, her heart melting that he remembered those moments. "It's been really hard, and I find myself sad sometimes, but I try my best." An occasional tear ran down her face, realizing Jesse only remembered the good things. Jesse ran his finger down Lizzie's hand and felt the geographic scars that now covered her skin.

"Does it hurt?" he asked curiously.

"My hand? No. My hand is healed, but I'll always have those bumps and scars. My stomach still hurts a lot, though. That's why I squealed a little bit when you tried to give me a hug. I'm sorry that scared you. I really want to give you the biggest hug in the entire world, but that probably won't be for a while," she explained. Jesse hung on to every word.

"Can I see?" he asked. Lyla was listening in to the conversation and looked over to see Lizzie looking at her to help move the gown out of the way. She carefully removed the blankets to one side of the bed and helped gently lift the gown off her skin. Soon, Lizzie's exposed stomach could be seen by her little brother, and he looked at the red, scarred skin, confused by this new world he was seeing. He reached his hand to touch it, but Lizzie was able to grab his hand before he touched the bare, exposed skin. She slowly guided his hand to areas of her stomach that were a little more healed and less painful. A couple of tears started to squeeze themselves out of Jesse's eyes, and Lizzie told him it was going to be okay. Lyla asked if they wanted a moment, and Lizzie nodded, suggesting they have a minute, just the two of them. Lyla mentioned she would go and tell the parents and Sophie.

"Why did they have to hurt you?" Jesse asked innocently.

"No one hurt me, Jesse. There was an accident, and I had to help a couple of kids and make sure they were okay," Lizzie explained. "I will be okay; it's just going to take some time to get better."

"How long? I miss you. I wanna play outside

and go on adventures with you," Jesse mentioned. Lizzie's heart broke, realizing what she had to tell him next.

"Jesse, our adventures will have to be a little different," she started to explain. Jesse looked at her confused, not knowing that his sister was about to say. "My legs won't work right anymore. I can't walk, so if and when I get out of this bed, I will have to use a wheelchair."

"You can't walk?" Jesse asked, his confused face tilted to the side, eyebrows furrowed. "Did you forget? I can teach you. It's easy."

"It… it won't work that way, Jesse. I remember how to walk, but my legs won't work. Do you know how if your controllers get disconnected, they don't work?" she explained. Jesse nodded his head in understanding. "Well sometimes, if someone gets into a really bad accident, the power cord that runs the legs gets disconnected, and then they don't work anymore."

"Can the doctor plug it back in?" Jesse asked.

"Not these plugs. Sometimes they are torn and broken, so they can't be fixed. There are some people that were able to fix them on their own after a LOOOOOTTT of work, but it has to come with a miracle," Lizzie explained.

"Where do miracles come from? I want one, so I can give it to you, and turn your legs back on," Jesse mentioned sweetly.

"I don't know. Sometimes people find them, sometimes they're lost forever. I'll do my absolute best to try to find one, but until then, I get to use a wheelchair to move around," Lizzie promised.

"Okay…" Jesse said. He sat and thought for a moment. "Can I ride in your wheelchair?"

"Yes Jesse, you can ride in my wheelchair," Lizzie agreed while chuckling. Jesse congratulated himself in excitement, and Lyla opened the door slowly to ask if they were ready for everyone to come back in. Lizzie nodded her head, and the nurse left to get everyone. Jesse stared at Lizzie for a moment until she caught his eye.

"What are you looking at, dude?" Lizzie asked.

"Your face. You still look like Lizzie. You're still my sister," Jesse answered with all sincerity.

"You think so? I have a lot of scars that make me look weird. Sometimes I wonder if I look like a monster," Lizzie answered while pointing at the biggest scar that covered half of her left cheek. "You stopped and stared when you first came in. I thought it scared you."

"You don't look like a monster. You look like my sister," he said confidently while holding her hand. She pulled his hand to her face to kiss it as everyone started shuffling back into the room. Sophie returned to her previous seat next to the other side of Lizzie's bed. Holly and Mark stood behind Jesse, holding each other's hand, and Leslie stood at the foot of the bed. After an awkward moment of silence, Leslie cleared her throat.

LESLIE

"Since everyone is here, I guess I do have some crazy news to reveal to you all," she started, motioning jazz hands with her arms. "I've been working with a group of people on the case for Mr. Davidson," she started to announce cheerfully. "The trials are going to take a while, so in order to give all that I can to help in this investigation, I have sold the house and will be moving to the state capital in a couple weeks. Isn't that exciting?!" Shock and deadly silence filled the faces of everyone in the room; everyone was rendered speechless by the announcement.

"We're… moving?" Jesse asked, heartbroken at the thought of leaving. He hopped off the stool he was sitting on and walked to the foot of the bed.

"Well, I'm moving. If you want to come, you can," Leslie answered sweetly, walking her way in his direction.

"No, Jesse can stay with me as long as he needs or wants," Mark interrupted as he stood in between them. "These kids need stability. So, what is this really about, Leslie? You're leaving your children behind for what… press attention? You do realize Lizzie won't be in here forever, right?"

"I'll be back by the time she gets out, she'll be fine," she tried to refute. She tried to go on, but couldn't get a word in.

"No. Trials like that take months, even up to a year," Mark started. "You are abandoning your younger children for the attention of being on camera, and it is despicable. You're not going." Holly grabbed his arm as he started to drift closer to his ex-wife. Lizzie pressed the call button, which emitted a high-pitched ring, to get everyone's attention. All eyes went to Lizzie.

"You sold the house?" she asked emotionally, keeping hold of Jesse's hand as he walked back over to her. Lyla peeked in the room and Lizzie shook her head to tell her she wasn't needed.

"Yep! I put some of the earnings in the bank for you and Jesse's education and expenses, but we'll be able to start over when I get back," Leslie explained cheerfully.

"Start over?" Lizzie repeated, perplexed. "Why do we need to start over?"

"A little chunk of change saved in the bank is supposed to make them feel better for losing the only home they have ever known?" Sophie interrupted. "Where is Lizzie supposed to go once she gets out of the hospital, since it sounds like you won't be back?" she stated while glancing at her father, implying his previous remark.

"She's not going," Mark refused.

"She will stay with us," Holly stated in a defensive tone. "We can take care of her for as long as she needs or wants." Mark looked to Holly, nodded his head in agreement, then turning to look at his bed-ridden daughter and putting his hand on Jesse's shoulder.

"Lizzie's going to live with us?!" Jesse barked in excitement. "Lizzie! You can come live with us!" Lizzie smiled and squeezed her brother's hand. She then looked back to her mother.

"Are you going to come back and visit before

I leave the hospital?" she asked quietly.

"I don't know. It's getting busy, but I will try," Leslie replied.

"That's not enough, Mom," Sophie busted in. "That's a political answer that you give to your constituents or people on the news. Not the vague, easily broken promise that you give to your own daughter. She needs that promise. She needs her fucking mother."

"Sophie," Mark interrupted. "Please calm down. I am as angry as you are, if not more. We will get through this and figure this out, but we need to stay calm." He looked over to Lizzie. "Whether your mom wants to be involved in your lives is up to her, but I will be here to support all three of you. Holly and I both. I know I haven't always been the most connected father, but the last few months have reminded me what is truly important. I need to be here for you kids." Everyone looked to Leslie for her response, only to see her look at her phone and down to her watch.

"Well, I have to head out. It's a long drive to the capital, and my car is waiting outside," she announced. She walked over to hug Sophie, who pushed her away in disgust. She kissed Lizzie's head, who sat in disbelief that her mother was just leaving. Jesse ran around the bed and hugged his mother, asking her to stay and not go while he fought back tears. She gave him a bear hug and a kiss, only to stand and wave a quiet goodbye to Holly and Mark. She walked out the door in silence. Time froze inside that crowded hospital room as everyone stood in disbelief, still in shock over what just happened that afternoon; they sat and tried to comprehend what all of it meant.

MARK

Jesse put his arms around Sophie's hips and asked when their mom was coming back.

"I don't know, Jesse. I don't know," was her only reply. She wiped a loose tear from his cheek.

"Lizzie, honey," Holly said, walking up to the bed and running her fingers through her hair. "How are you doing, my sweet girl?"

"I don't know," Lizzie answered. "I don't know what to think right now. What am I going to do? It feels like as time goes by, more and more of my life has to start over."

"We will be here to help you, okay? We are right here and always will be," Holly started to answer. Mark continued to stand behind her, a subtle tear falling from his eye as he watched the love of his life comforting his heartbroken daughter. "Sophie," Holly said, ushering her to hold hands. "We will be here for all three of you. I love you girls," she glanced over at Jesse peaking above the bed, "and boy... with all my heart. You are my babies. Do not ever forget that, okay?" she preached, while exchanging looks with all the kids. Sophie sent a mischievous look to her father, confirming to him that she was the one. Mark caught the look, smiled and nodded; he walked to the foot of the bed and watched his little family support each other as he thought about what he wanted to say. He ushered Holly over to him to tell her something.

"How are we going to do this? We can't fit everyone in that apartment," he mentioned.

"We'll figure it out, but these kids need us. They need you," Holly said with encouragement.

Holly rolled a table up to the bed as Sophie helped Jesse jump into the bed with Lizzie. Lyla walked into the room announcing it was her lunch break and asked if everyone was ready for a card game. She shuffled the cards on the table and dealt 5 cards to everyone standing around. Chris put his feet up on the couch near the window and checked his phone; Mark took charge of the armchair near the bed and opened his laptop to check his work emails. Lyla explained the rules, and warned the participants that Lizzie had an impressive game, so beware of her skills. Jesse held the cards for Lizzie as she told him which to keep and which to give away. After winning almost every game, Jesse high-fived his big sister and jumped off the bed to tell his father about his wins. Lyla gave everyone hugs before she left to check back in and make her rounds to her other patients. Mark stood to pick up his son and walked over to the foot of the bed. After asking everyone else how the games went, he cleared his throat.

"So, today was not the day that anyone expected," he started. "Holly is right. We will be here to support all three of you through anything. I will be here for all of you," he said as he walked over to Holly and grabbed her hands. "Holly, you have changed my entire world, and you've helped me remember what is actually important in my life. You've taken my kids as your own, which is more than I could ever ask. You've been so patient through this crisis. You've shown me what love does look like, and I don't want those smiles to end, Holly. What would you say about us growing old together?" he stopped. Holly looked at him confused for a moment.

"Wait. What?" she asked, trying to figure out what he was trying to say.

"Holly, in the presence of all three of my

children… well… our children…. I wanted to ask you if you will marry me," he admitted, while dropping to his knee and grabbing the small box out of his front pocket. Holly squealed in excitement as she realized what was happening. Jesse ripped his hand from Lizzie's and jumped up and down. Sophie and Lizzie let out a synchronized awwwwwe at the news. Holly picked Mark up off the floor.

"Of course, I will."

Hearing

LIZZIE

I laid in my hospital bed and watched as the entire room was enveloped with beautiful, jovial emotions over the proposal. Holly has been such a good person to be around, and she was probably the best person I could ask for to marry my dad. Tears welled up in my eyes and sat in the grooves of my facial scars. I almost had to punch Sophie to get her attention in order to grab a towel for me to wipe the pools off my face. I told Holly to get her butt over here so I could see the ring, which was absolutely stunning. One larger stone in the middle, and two smaller stones, one on either side. I grabbed her hand and slid my thumb over the ring, feeling the proposal on my fingertips. Jesse was jumping for joy, almost to the point of bouncing off the walls. Dad and Holly tried to calm him down, but there was no stopping this hyper-energized nine-year old from destroying everything in the room. Sophie asked Holly if she wanted to go with her go get treats for the special occasion, and Holly suggested they take Jesse with them to get him out of the room.

"Mark, are you okay to stay here?" Holly asked with happy tears still dropping from her cheek. My heart melted with all the emotions everyone was experiencing.

"Of course, you guys have fun. My card is in the middle console of the Benz. Let me pay for the treats," Dad replied with a wink. Holly and Sophie nodded in agreement as they ushered the pepped-up Jesse out the door and into the hallway. Dad sat in the chair next to my bed where Jesse had been sitting, and there was quite the awkward silence as I could tell he was trying to find the right words to say.

"Dad, you okay?"

"Ya, ya. I'm fine," he replied, still pondering his next words. "I know I owe you a lot of explanations, but I just don't know where to start," he started to explain.

"Dad, don't worry about it. There's nothing to explain. I'm just glad you're here. That's all that matters," I said as I tried to comfort him.

"No. I needed to be here with you. That's not fair that your mother wasn't here as much as I thought she was. I know it has taken me almost four months to finally get up here. Honestly," he started as he grabbed both her hands. "I was scared. I was scared to see my baby girl in pain. I saw you that first day, the fresh burns and the blood... a... and... I couldn't do it. I also didn't think you would want to see me because I have been distant lately with you and Jesse. However, it kills me that you have been here alone. I can't imagine how scary and lonely that must have been," he explained. A part of me shattered, realizing how serious he was and seeing the fear that exuded from his face. He had been one of the biggest examples of rock-hard strength in my life, so to see him being this vulnerable shocked me more than anything.

"It's been okay. Lyla has pretty much followed me to wherever I was moved, so she's become a pretty good friend," I explained while peeking out the door. "Dad, I didn't know you were feeling all of that. I'm so sorry."

"You shouldn't be the one that is sorry, Lizzie..."

"Dad?" I asked. He lifted his head to look at me face-to-face. I could see he was choking back tears. "I'm ecstatic about you and Holly. You are really cute together," I said upliftingly. I guess that comment got to him, because it sure brought a smile to his face.

"I'm glad you say that. I wanted to ask you first, but obviously, things didn't go as planned," he replied, hinting at Mom's appearance.

"She's been confusing me, lately. She's changed a lot in the past few weeks. Have you seen that?" I asked him. He nodded in disappointment, the fact that he had seen it too. "She was here all the time at first, but she started fighting with the doctors and nurses more and more because they weren't doing enough. And then, she just stopped coming," I started explaining. "And now she sold the house? And pretty much just picked up and left? I understand a lot of things pretty well, but I don't know what's going on in her head anymore."

"I know. I think we all have a case of whiplash from the past few months," he started. I nodded my head in understanding and snickered at the comparison. "It shouldn't have to be your job to understand her. What you need, what all of you need, is stability and familiarity, now more than ever. I know it's harder said than done, and both you girls do this, but please try to do your best to focus on your own healing, okay? And know that Holly and I are here. You focus as much as you can on being a kid, a teenager. You've grown, way too fast." Dad combed his fingers through my hair. "I am incredibly proud of you, Lizzie."

"Thank you, Dad. It looks like we all are going to learn a lot in the near future," I commented sarcastically. We chuckled together at the thought of our new lives; at the same time, I could hear a rambunctious child jumping around and talking at speeds barely heard by adults. "I think they're back," I mentioned as I pointed to the door. Jesse came running in at the speed of light, his arms stretched out as he pretended to fly like an airplane.

"Yoooooooo guess what?! We got ice cream!" he growled in overwhelming excitement. He jumped into Dad's arms still pretending to be a plane. I had to laugh at his childish glee. It was nice to see this much happiness after everything that just happened with Mom. Sophie and Holly grabbed the ice cream sandwiches out of the shopping bag and passed them around. I watched Holly walk out the door and get my doctor's attention. I could see just enough out the window that she was talking about me. She pointed in my direction a couple times during the short conversation, and after he nodded, she came walking back in.

"Guess what? Lizzie gets to have one, too!" Holly announced, opening the wrapper partway and handing me my own ice cream. We hounded Holly about what she wanted her future wedding to look like, and Jesse went on about how excited he was that I was moving in with them after I left the hospital. Any mention of my mom was internally banned from this conversation; there was too much happiness at risk.

"Congratulations, everyone! I just heard the good news!" Lyla proclaimed as she walked into the room to check on me. She snuck behind the crowd to get to my IVs to check if anything needed filled. "Lizzie, did you tell these guys about your first wheelchair ride? I mean, it was a lot, but... it's still good news." Everyone turned to me, expecting me to tell the story. I rolled my eyes at Lyla and glared at her slightly.

"I finally convinced the doctor to let me out of the bed. It was only for a second, but I was finally out," I stated. Holly jumped to my bedside and grabbed my hand.

"And how did it go? What did she mean when she said it was a lot?" Holly asked gently, slight concern in her voice. Her eyes bounced between Lyla and me.

"This was a month ago. The skin on my back was... and is... still healing, so everything was tight and sensitive and excruciatingly painful when the nurses picked me up to put me in the wheelchair. It reminded me a lot of the accident." As I explained the experience, I started to shut down and get a little quieter and more reserved. To say that I was emotionally scarred from what I had been through the last few months was a vast understatement; it was even harder to re-live as I tried to hide how vulnerable I felt explaining this to everyone. I saw a couple smiles of sympathy from Sophie and Lyla, but everyone else clung on to my every word. Dad squeezed my hand as he got ready to give another speech. Holly grabbed a tissue from the table next to my bed and wiped away a couple tears that I didn't realize were squeezing themselves out of my eyes.

"I'm happy you were able to get out of the bed, even though it was really painful," he told me as he put his hand around my cheek. "If you decide to do it again, let me know, okay? I want to be a part of your recovery from now on. I'm here to support you" I looked around the room to see Holly and Sophie nodding their heads. A sudden silence filled the room. I knew what they were thinking. The last time I got out of this bed was traumatizing. "Did I want to do that again? I know I've healed more since then, but do I really want to put myself through that? I held on to Dad's hand tightly as I thought about what I wanted to do. I wanted to, but did I really want to?"

"You'll really be here, Dad?" I asked

hesitantly, still nervous and in deep thought.

"Yes, of course. You can trust me." He leaned over and kissed my hand. My lips pursed to one side as I continued to think. Lyla stood in the background listening in, biting her lip and watching to see what I was going to decide. After what seemed like an hour of awkward silence, but was probably only 60 seconds, I asked Lyla if she would help. She nodded quickly and ran to get a wheelchair to bring in. Sophie and Holly helped me take the hoard of blankets off my body, and Jesse ran to Dad's side. Lyla came back in with the wheelchair and said it would be a minute until the physical therapist would have a moment to come help. Dad interrupted her and asked if he could be the one to lift me out of the bed, and she could follow closely behind in case anything bad happened. She agreed but asked that the physical therapist came in to watch and give input. She set the locks on the wheelchair and walked over to the sink to grab a towel for me to place in my mouth. Dad and Jesse looked confused about the towel, and Lyla explained that they would understand when it was relevant. The physical therapist came in not too long after, and Lyla relayed the plan.

Holly ushered Jesse to come and stand near her so Dad and Lyla could have more room. Dad stood up and moved the chair he was sitting in, and Lyla slid in behind the IV stand. Dad slid his arms under my knees and back, and he braced himself to hold my weight. I couldn't really feel pain in the skin on my thighs due to the paralysis, but my back still felt like tape was being ripped from my skin. I was able to lift my arm around his neck, squealing in muffled pain as he lifted my body from the bed and carried me to the wheelchair. The pain was intense. I could feel how tight my skin had gotten from months of recovery and sitting in bed. Tears slid down my face as Dad gently dropped me in the wheelchair, grabbing my arms immediately and holding me in a bear hug as I felt what it was like to finally sit up. The pain was excruciating enough, I started to see bright lights again, and I almost passed out.

Jesse ran to my side and held my hand as tears streamed down my face. I continued to breakdown from the pain of my tightened, still healing skin. Dad started to put his arms beneath me to pick me back up, but I shook my head and refused. I needed to feel this. I needed to feel what it was like to sit up, to feel somewhat normal in my new normal existence. The physical therapist watched, intensely concentrated to make sure nothing went awry. Holly and Sophie also surrounded me and kept telling me it was going to be okay, and wiped tears from my face. Lyla kept asking me if I needed anything or if it was time to move me back to the bed, but I wanted to continue to hold on as long as I could. After a couple minutes of sitting in the wheelchair, the physical therapist said that was probably enough and that I needed to be moved back to the bed. Dad nodded his head, and he quickly but gently scooped me up and carried me back to the bed. Holly and Sophie covered me back up with blankets as the nurse put medication into my IV. A now tearful Jesse ran to my bedside and held my hand to his face, hugging what he could of me as I tried to calm myself from the pain.

No one left my room until I had stopped tearing up and was able to breathe again. They kept telling me how well I did and how proud of me they were. I smiled timidly as I continued to pick up my emotional pieces and put them back together. Dad slid his hand over my hair and told me that he would be here whenever I decided I wanted to do this again, and Jesse continued to tell me that I didn't need to cry and that everything was okay. Today couldn't have been any better. That intimate moment of everyone being there to help me get back into the wheelchair is something that I knew I would always hold super special. Even though the news of Mom selling the house and moving was devastating, I was still able to see the happiness on my family's faces from the events that followed her exit.

Doctor James walked in shortly after Dad got me back to my bed. He seemed a little more "up" than usual, which only added more excitement to the atmosphere.

"I noticed that you tried out the chair again. Did it go better this time?" he asked, with a somewhat snarky tone. I wiped a leftover tear off my face and replied that it did go a lot better. He noticed the physical therapist still standing in the corner talking to Lyla. The physical therapist nodded in agreement. Doctor James checked out the scars that were developing on my back and asked how I felt about it. I was really confused about this question. I asked him to repeat that question.

"I wanted to ask how it went, because I think you are finally healed enough to start more challenging physical therapy, and perhaps to get you out and about now," he explained. My eyes nearly popped out of my head because of what he just said, and I went to hug him before flopping back into the bed with pain from stretching my skin too far. I went on and on about how excited I was to finally get out of this damn bed. The doctor soon lost my attention because I was surrounded by Holly and Sophie talking about how excited they were. In the distance, I saw Dad pull him aside and talk to him about something. I didn't care what, but there was a smile on his face, so it must have been good. I couldn't wait for my life to change again, this time for the better.

Dad came back over to join the crowd,

grabbed my hand, and said:

"I will be here. Every step of the way."

LIZZIE

My medications still made my dreams unbelievably vivid. That night was no different. My eyes squinted as I stared into the sky, the sun's rays beaming upon the park. It was a perfect, cloudless day except for the 32-degree temperature tightening the skin on my face. It was a short walk to the park from my house, but the trek was worth it for the room that there was to create the snowball fight of the century for Jesse. I couldn't count the number of times I passed his room and witnessed him with poster boards on the ground drawing out his strategies. I couldn't understand the red marker scrapings flying across the paper surface, but anytime I looked, he yelled at me to walk away and not to tell anybody his plan. I didn't know what he was talking about, but I obliged to his request. I saw nothing.

Sophie and I stood next to a towering willow tree, protecting ourselves from the elements and waited for Jesse to create his fighting ground for the battle. He demanded 30 minutes to be set aside for him and Sophie's kids to build their empire before us big people destroyed their hopes and dreams. Sophie had just moved to her current home, which was a lot farther away from her apartment that she and Chris shared for a couple years. I insisted she show me pictures of the house made up, since it was hard for us to make the trip to see them with me not having my driver's license yet and Mom always at work. She continued to cringe at the towers of boxes that were still scattered all over the house, but she flipped through countless pictures of the kids' rooms all set up, the spacious great room with deep vaulted ceilings and columns draping to the ground, and the adorable playhouse in the backyard that Chris made for the girls. Sophie kept talking about what projects she was planning next, and how excited she was to host Christmas this year.

Out of nowhere, a snowball exploded over the back of my shoulder. I turn to see Jesse giggling to himself while covering his face. He announced that his territory was ready for war and ran to the huge mound of snow that he built with his nieces and nephew. Sophie and I huddled together and talked about our strategy, and then just started picking up snow and forming it into balls at factory speed. Once the kids braced themselves for impact, I started chucking the snowballs at the make-shift fort until a cloud of snow filled the air from the impact. Sophie snuck away from the tree and around the cloud of frozen water particles to create a flank. Then at the count of three, we both charged at the helpless children until we met in the middle with a huge group hug, lifting the children out of the mount and taking over the kingdom that they had built. Children screams followed, as the towering giants took over their hard work. They raided the castle, throwing anything that they could find: snowballs, pinecones, hats from each other's heads. The next thing I knew, I woke up from the dream that had my attention for so long.

LIZZIE

Back into reality, I was, in that quiet, dreary hospital bed without the ability to walk. Dad walked in and took off his tie, setting his stuff on the sofa in the far corner of the room. He asked me how I was, and I talked about the dream that I had. After having what seemed like the same dream for weeks, I started to feel frustrated and disappointed that I wouldn't be able to walk and run around anymore. I was starting to feel empty again, more like a burden than an actual human being. Dad sat and listened to my thoughts, holding my hands and replying with understanding nods. He still sucked at talking about emotion too much, so I wasn't expecting him to say anything profound, or anything at all. It just felt better to have someone else to listen.

Lyla came in shortly after seeing Dad arrive. She asked how ready I was to get into the wheelchair. I had been able to build up my endurance and pain tolerance enough to sit in the wheelchair for almost a half an hour, which meant that I was able to adventure out of my room and into the world of freedom, even if it was for a few minutes. Lyla set the brakes on the wheelchair as Dad moved the blankets to put his arms under my back. I cringed from my pulling skin as Dad lifted my weight and carried me to the chair. I laid back into the chair to relax a little bit. Rolling up his sleeves, Dad grabbed the handles of the chair and started to wheel me around the room, only to be stopped by Lyla, who was trying to undo all the cords from my IV's.

"Patience, my lovelies. Let's not strangle her," she muffled.

I wanted to go outside of the hospital this time, out into the fresh air; I wanted to see the sun and feel the rays on my face. I asked Dad where we needed to go, and he guided us to the elevator to carry us five floors down. Surreal was the only feeling washing through my body when the bells of the elevator kept announcing which floor we were on. After dropping to the ground floor, Dad wheeled me through the Lobby and out the front entrance. Sun rays had to be scratched out of the plan since the day was cloudy, but I still sat and breathed deep breaths of fresh oxygen into my body. I felt Dad's hand on my shoulder as I just sat and stared at the swaying trees, feeling the cool breeze on my face. Lyla jumped in front of me with an extra blanket to put over myself if I got cold. I was chilled, but I didn't want the blanket. The feeling of the real world on my skin grounded me and gave me a new-found sense of liveliness about life. I felt a glimpse of what I'd been dreaming about for months. Freedom… Freedom!

40 minutes later, Dad carried me to my bed as I cringed in searing pain from my chilled skin tightening around me. Lyla tucked the warm blankets around my body, and then she hustled to the nurse's station to grab some medication. Even though I was worlds better from where I was, I was still having a hard time with the pain. Agonizing tears pried themselves from my tear ducts. Lyla rushed around the bed to re-adjust the IV's, and Dad simply sat next to the bed and held my hand as he wiped some of the moisture off my face. He half smiled and looked down, unable to know what to say to make me feel better. I slowly turned my body to see him. I didn't know what to think anymore. "I should be able to do this. Why can't I do more?" My heart broke more and more as I thought about it. Being trapped in that state had become so discouraging. I just felt stuck.

"This sucks."

"I know, I'm sorry." Dad continued to look down. "I know I've only been here a short bit of your recovery, but I see a little bit of what you're up against, and it kills me that I can't take it away from you."

"There's nothing you have to be sorry about, Dad. This whole situation just sucks. I'm just happy to have someone here. I love Lyla and all, but… I spent a lot of time alone before this. It's just nice to feel that support." We sat in sobering thought for a few moments, unsure of what to talk about. Dad mentioned that the first hearing for the superintendent was being televised and asked me if I wanted to watch. I thought about it for a moment. I was still deeply hurt about Mom's departure, but my curiosity of what could happen to Mr. Davidson overshadowed that. I nodded my head, and Dad turned the TV on and flipped through channels until he found the right news station.

It was Mom's station. They just announced that she was no longer with the station and wished her luck in her future endeavors. Our heads cocked to the side, confused that Mom's job that she loved so much was no longer. Yet another moment of whiplash that Mom was putting everyone through. "What does this mean?"

With a blink of an eye, the station cut to a shot of the front entrance of the state house, which was crowded with people protesting outside. I sat up in my bed, still trying to comprehend what I just heard. Looking over at Dad, I saw him tapping his forehead with the remote, his left-hand white knuckling the chair's armrest. I tapped his hand repeatedly to get his attention, but the shade of red in his face deepened. The sounds of chants from the protests echoed from the TV. Time stood still as I watched my dad slowly implode, but I had to get his attention. I grabbed an extra towel that laid on a table on my other side and tried to toss it in front of his face. My aim failed, and the towel struck him in the eye. Dad caught it as it dropped to his lap and threw it hard against the wall on the other side of the room. He stood up quickly, tossing the remote into the seat behind him, and started pacing back and forth across the room grumbling to himself. I waved my arm as far as I could, but nothing could get his attention.

"Dad…. Daaaad…. DAADD!" Dad stopped where he was and finally looked in my direction. "Dad, what's going on? Are you okay?"

"Uhm… yes… uhm… sorry Lizzie," he apologized. He stood there at the foot of my bed for a minute to stretch his muscles, and then came back over to the armchair and sat back down.

"You freaked me out for a minute, Dad. You zoned out. Your face looked like a tomato people throw at comics that aren't funny. Will you tell me what's going on?" I asked with concern.

"I really am sorry, Lizzie. I guess hearing about your mom quitting her job really got to me." He slid his fingers through his hair and rubbed his face.

"Why?" I asked.

"I really shouldn't be bringing drama in with your mom. But… I remember when we were still together, and this was all your mom cared about… this job," he explained. "She did everything she could do to get that job, and no one was getting in her way. Not even me… it wasn't the only reason for the split, but it was unfortunately a big part of it."

"Dad… I… I'm sorry. I didn't know," I tried to explain.

"You guys were kids. You didn't need to know all the adult things that were happening."

"I mean… it's hard not to be when it ends up being a divorce," I replied. "But I kind of understand what you mean. I almost wonder if Grandma Faulkner got in the way too. That's around the same time Mom sent her away."

"I heard about that. That was around the same time, wasn't it?" Dad asked rhetorically. I nodded my head and we sat in quiet thought for a moment. He decided we didn't need to sit in on the hearing and turned off the TV. He asked if it was okay that he did some work on his laptop for a bit before the doctor came in, and I agreed. I was exhausted, so I laid back and let my eyes rest for a while.

Later that day, Lyla surprised me with an announcement that she was able to coordinate another video call with Grandma. She pulled the table over to the bed and sat her bright red laptop computer on its surface. After a couple minutes of clicks and navigating, I saw Grandma's nose in the camera. She was still learning what technology was about, and I guess video-calling was no different. After telling her a couple times that she could have the camera farther away from her face, the nurse on the other end offered to hold the phone for her so she could focus on talking. I thanked the nurse for her help, and asked Grandma how she was doing. After her trailing off for a minute about what activities she was up to, she paused and looked into the camera. She stared intently on what I could only assume was my face, which was still severely scarred and deformed in some places.

"What are you looking at, Grandma?" I asked.

"Something is different about you, dear."

"It's probably the scars. I still have a lot of healing to do, and my face is always going to look a little different," I tried to explain. Grandma still sat in deep thought with her hand on her chin. She tilted her head.

"There's something different." Everyone paused on both ends, confused about what she meant. Was this her dementia kicking in? Was she having a harder time recognizing me? "You don't seem yourself, baby girl. Are you doing okay?"

"What do you mean, Grandma? I'm okay. Everything just hurts a little bit, and I'm really tired."

"I can see through those eyes. Something is bothering you. It's hurting you," she said. I could see her usher the nurse to bring the phone closer so she could see easier. I took a deep swallow, knowing I couldn't hide from her.

"Grandma," I started, resituating myself so I was sitting up a little higher. "It's been hard. I can't walk anymore, and I can't do a lot for myself. Dad's been here more, but I feel like I should be better by now. Can I ask you something?" Grandma nodded her head with that sweet, comforting smile. "Do you ever feel like you are a burden to people around you?" Both the rooms we were in went quiet. The silence was deafening.

"Sweetie, sometimes we want to do so much more than we are able," she advised. "The important thing to remember, is that sometimes we need to accept a little bit of help." She picked up a photo from her stand and tried to show me through the phone. It took some configuring, but I was able to see a chubby, blonde baby, sitting next to a sofa. "Do you know who this is?"

"I think that's me?" I said, not confident. Dad looked into the phone and nodded in confirmation that it was me as a little one.

"I remember this little baby," she said, pointing at the photo. "Your mom was so excited that you sat yourself up at such a young age. You were so smart." I started to smile at her compliments. "This baby is up to amazing things. She will learn a lot, and she will help a lot of people. She just has to remember how strong she is and gifted she is. There's nothing she can't do." I muttered "except for walk" under my breath, but it was still loud enough that Dad nudged my arm and whispered for me to listen. "This is a determined little girl, and so are you." She looked back at me and told me to remember what she said. After promising through the phone, the call had to be cut short so she could go eat. What does determined really mean to me?

LESLIE

Leslie and Emily walked up the steps to the state house in nervous excitement. They had been preparing for this day for months and were confident they would be able to make headway in the case. Leslie made the official move, and Emily drove in two days before to help consolidate all the information she had gathered from the parent group. Protesters had already started to line up, some for the case, and some against. Shouts echoed as they met Matt at the entrance. Awkward side hugs and handshakes aside, they followed each other inside the foyer and through the hallways towards an empty meeting room that was reserved for them to gather their beginning strategies.

"Soooooo, I've gathered the lists," Emily started. "And we have 16,587 signatures! We've really been stretching our resources, so I don't know for sure how many more we can get here on out." She placed stacks and stacks of petition forms on the table. Matt congratulated her on the accomplishment of getting so many signatures and announced that they were able to gather dozens of stories of mistreatment ranging from racial slurs, misogynistic and depraved remarks to his admins and secretaries, to income shaming and public humiliation of students. He wished them all luck as they embarked on the treacherous journey of fighting for this little-known, rural school district.

The sounds of their heels clicking on the marbled floors echoed through the tall, Greek-style atrium of the state house as they walked their way to the legislative chamber where the hearing was scheduled. Rumbles of distant conversation reverberated through the hallways as Leslie and Emily passed countless well-groomed men in shiny black suits. At the end of the hallway, two massive, towering oak doors awaited their arrival. The hinges creaked with age as Matt pushed his way into the chambers, Emily and Leslie closely behind. The room echoed every voice that spoke, and an old, musty odor emanated from the carpets. Aged portraits of history covered the walls of the antiquated room.

Matt guided the women to their seats on the left side of the room. Across the walkway were five men in snappy suits and slicked back hair, standing in a circle mumbling together. As people started to file in, news crews started trying to occupy the entrance, soon to be pushed away by security. Leslie and Emily listened as protesters started chanting louder and louder outside. They turned to look behind them to see Superintendent Davidson arrogantly swaggering his way through the atrium and into the room. He met the five men in suits, shaking hands, and confidently adjusting his tie and putting his suit coat back on. He fastened his cufflinks as he watched behind him, all the people that were here to see the hearing take place. The five men, presumed to be his lawyers at this point, guided him to an armchair near their table, and all took their seats. With the looks of their freshly shined shoes and the glare from their gold watches blinding Leslie in the face, Mr. Davidson spared no expense on hiring the best. "Where did the money come from? Surely, he didn't pay for it himself."

Matt nudged Emily, who nudged Leslie, who all turned to the front of the room to see the members of the Department of Education filing in and taking their own seats. The room started to quiet down, and hushed whispers echoed through the chamber. After all members had taken their seats, the representative sitting in the middle of them all stood and announced the beginning of the hearing.

Soon, the representative gave the time over for beginning remarks. The Davidson team was up first.

"Ladies and gentlemen of the board, in the proceedings of these hearings, we plan to show the impact that Superintendent Davidson has made with the school district. We plan to prove that the intentions behind the prosecuting team is not for the good of the public, and that these proceedings are only for personal gain…" After about 10 minutes of preaching, the attorney continued with his goals of the defense, and turned the time over to Matt.

"Good morning, members of the board. I am happy to be here with you all today. Happy to finally take part in holding this man accountable for his actions as superintendent," he turned and directed attention to Mr. Davidson himself. "As a trusted member of the community who has also had children graduate through the district, I will reveal to you all the cases of gross, and despicable mistreatment towards not only co-workers and confidants, but to students as well. We will uncover cases of mishandling of funds, bordering on the crime of embezzlement, as well as foul, disgusting neglect of school infrastructure which directly contributed to severe building and property management and almost caused a tragic death of one of my colleague's children. This man should not be in the education field, nor should he be in charge of protecting our children and community. He needs to be held accountable for his INACTION, and we need to stand up for the real heroes in the classroom, the teachers that have spent countless hours and their own funds to continue teaching, while Mr. Davidson continues to refuse to give them a proper place to teach and learn."

Matt continued to go on and on in his summary about what he and Leslie's team had been finding, mentioning more neglect of the buildings, noting Mr. Davidson's tenure and longevity, whilst also continuing to abuse his power as superintendent, and connecting that it was the duty of the board to not fail the children of the school district. After a half an hour of introductory remarks, the board set a short recess for both sides to continue to bring together their cases. Leslie and Emily both fidgeted in their chairs, finally realizing how real this experience was and was going to be, and anxious how this would pan out.

SOPHIE

Sophie walked into the nursing home nervously, eyeing the many patients that were out for a stroll or playing cards in the great room. The sun shone harshly through the building windows, and the hallway seemed so much longer than it used to be. She felt guilty that it has been so long since she had come to visit, but since Lizzie was sleeping right now, and physical therapy wasn't until that afternoon, she decided this was the best time as any. As she walked into her great-grandmother's room, she grasped the reality of how long it had been since she had come. It appeared that her great grandma had lost another 20 pounds, and her face had started to sink in and discolor slightly.

They greeted with a warm embrace, and Sophie sat in patience as she felt her grandmother's hands feel the shape of her face and shoulders. She asked how Sophie had been doing. Sophie talked about the kids, and the firsts that they had started experiencing. She talked about Chris being promoted at work, and how he was travelling a lot more, so they had started considering getting a new place closer to his job, and to give them more room for the kids to grow. She updated her about the family; that Jesse had moved in with their father, and Lizzie was healing well in the hospital and had more physical therapy. She then mentioned that their mother had sold the house and moved to the state capital for the hearings but tried to leave out the matter of how she announced she was leaving. She talked about how chaotic life had continued to be, and how her mind wasn't able to calm down and enjoy the moment anymore. She asked her grandmother for advice, how to find peace in the world they were living in.

"I hear you, baby. When your great-grandfather and I were young, we lived through some really hard times. They rationed a lot of the food we could eat, and no one could build houses because the resources went to the soldiers. I had six kids to care for, all by myself, because your grandpa had decided to enlist and fight. I spent a lot of time angry at him and the world. Nothing ever slowed down, and there were countless dinners I left myself out of so that my kids had something that day," Sophie put her arm around her grandma and laid her head on her shoulders. She became a little child again, craving safety and peace from the family matriarch as she went on.

"Sometimes there is nothing we can do to slow down the life we are living, but we need to focus on what matters the most. Some people may hurt us; sometimes life doesn't go our way; and sometimes we feel like there isn't enough we can do, but we need to remember that they aren't our circus. They aren't our monkeys. It's pretty hard, and it's easier said than done, but we have to remember we can't be in control of everything. Remember how strong you are. You're a Faulkner, even though your last name doesn't say so. We stubborn ladies need to remember what our circle of influence really is, and that we can change the world, even if it's only the world for the people that depend on us. You are strong. You are brave. You can do so much more than you give yourself credit for. All of us have those moments, but you will get through this." Grandma kissed Sophie on the forehead and wiped away the wandering tears that had trickled down her face. They sat in silence holding each other and leaning on each other's shoulders so Sophie could just feel the safety of her grandmother's arms. Grandma Faulkner rocked Sophie back and forth and started humming sweet lullabies to comfort her beloved great-granddaughter.

Soon, the stale, old bedroom became a warm, childhood playroom, filled with toys and stars and clouds, all floating around the two. Sophie remembered when Grandma read her stories, and she cuddled in her lap, rocking back and forth in the rocking chair and smelling the sweet lilac smell of Grandma's perfume wafting in the air. She remembered the sound of her child-like giggle as Grandma invented new character voices and her exaggerated expressions for each personality in the story. Grandma's voice transported Sophie into imaginary worlds full of color, flowers, trees, and rainbows around every turn. Story after story she told, filling Sophie's head with fairytales and legends, growing her young mind. Sophie wanted to stay in this state, forever.

TERROR

MARK

Mark and Holly packed up the remaining boxes from their rental as they prepared to move into a bigger place. Once they picked up the rest of Jessie's things from Leslie's house, they quickly realized that there was not enough room for Lizzie once she got out of the hospital. They also realized that she wouldn't be able to navigate the home with the narrow doorframes and cornered hallways with her wheelchair.

Boxes continued to pile up next to the front door. The moving truck was running late, so Holly set up a wall of boxes that were ready to move as soon as they arrived. Jesse ran around in circles in the empty great room with his arms stretched wide, racing imaginary airplanes in his way. Mark took a break to check his work emails and get ready for the next quarterly meeting. Profits were down slightly for the first time since he took his position, but he still carried the company through a rocky stock season, so he was confident that the meeting would go well. Juggling work, home, wedding planning, and taking care of both Jesse and Lizzie all took its toll on Mark. The sides of his hairline were slightly greyed, and the bags under his eyes had deepened. He laid his head on the kitchen island briefly to rest his eyes, only to be shaken awake by Holly a short time later so she could announce that the moving company had arrived. He ushered her away for a moment as he woke from the island, and he joined the rest of the group a couple moments later.

Holly lifted Jesse up to the moving truck so he could place the last box into the pile. It was official. Their lives at 87 Halogen Place were now packed into the back of a truck and saved as memories in their minds. They watched what was left of their possessions roll down the driveway and down the road; the reality set in that a new normal was about to set forth. Holly laid her head on Mark's shoulder to rest and think for a moment. Jesse ran off into the front yard on another airplane adventure to save his lost basketball. Mark asked Holly to imagine what life used to be like a few months ago. No kids, a quiet, clean, modern apartment…. The floor of the Benz was now covered in toys and old French fries. He talked about being in shock still, months after taking custody of Jesse and coming back to his hometown. He talked about how he never dreamed of being back, and that if she had asked him months ago if he thought he would be where he was, he would have never believed it. Holly put her arms around him and squeezed, watching the bright orange sun begin to set behind the other two-story homes in the cul-de-sac.

"Should we head to the new place?" she proposed. Mark nodded his head and turned to get the keys to the Benz. Holly called for Jesse, and they hopped into the car. She asked if he was ready to see the new house, and Jesse aggressively nodded his head in excitement. He yanked the seat belt to buckle in and struggled to find the buckle, attempting multiple times before finally hearing it clip. Mark did a final lock up of the front of the house and opened the car door. Before sitting down, he leaned in and asked everyone if they were ready. After seeing nods from everyone inside, he sat in the driver's seat and started up the car.

Off they went, 25 minutes away, to 68 Hopkins Street, a ranch-style two-story farmhouse just off the freeway. It was conveniently closer to Jesse's school and being so close to the freeway meant Mark had the access in case he needed to go to the office or save time driving to the hospital. The three-bedroom, three-bathroom home sported dark walnut beamed ceilings and was built for wheelchair access, thanks to the previous owners' health conditions. It was perfect for Lizzie and had even more room for Jesse to run around in his airplane battles. Everyone could now have their own space to grow and live.

Mark drove into the driveway and parked the Benz in front of the garage. The moving truck was parked to the right, closer to the front door, the crew had waited until they arrived before they started moving numerous boxes and belongings into the house. Holly took the keys from Mark and unlocked the door for the moving crew. Mark and Jesse stood on the front lawn together, Mark leaning over to tell Jesse about this house and how much room they had.

"Guess what the best part is, bud?" Mark asked curiously.

"What?! What?! Whaaaat?!"

"I bought this house. We won't need to move again. This is our home," he announced. Jesse smiled with his immense, child-like glee and wrapped his arms around Mark's legs. Holly met the boys on the lawn and asked what they were doing. After hearing that it was announced that this was the final move, Holly gave the boys a group hug and knelt to talk to Jesse. She asked if Jesse was excited for the new house, Jesse nodding excitedly and throwing himself around Holly's neck. Holly picked Jesse up off the ground and sat him on her hip, as she and Mark stared at their new future. After basking in a moment of excitement, they sat Jesse down, and gave him the freedom to run around outside while Mark and Holly went in to arrange boxes and help the moving crew finish up the work.

A few nights later, Mark and Holly woke up to the sound of Jesse screaming in his room downstairs. Worried for the worst, they flew down the stairs missing half the steps on the way down to see what was going on. Upon entering his room, they found Jesse swinging at an invisible force in mid-air. They had never seen this before. It was worse than any nightmare they had ever seen. Holly rushed over to grab Jesse before he jumped off his bed. Grabbing his sides, Holly didn't see Jesse's fist fly behind him and hit her in the nose and upper lip. Mark ran over and grabbed his arms, telling him repeatedly to wake up. Suddenly, the screaming stopped, and Jesse went motionless. They all sat down with caution, Holly reaching over and grabbing a tissue from the nightstand to stop the dreaded bleeding she could feel coming through her nasal cavity. Jesse looked around the dark room and asked what was going on. Confused, Mark and Holly sat there watching him.

"Wait, do you not remember anything?" Mark asked, perplexed at the chaos of what just happened. Jesse simply shook his head, and terrified tears ran down his face. Mark explained that Jesse started screaming bloody murder in the middle of the night, and they came into the room with him swinging his fists at something. Jesse withdrew into himself with guilt and embarrassment, but Holly simply hugged him and held on, whispering to him that it was going to be okay. That everyone was okay. Jesse leaned into her chest and sobbed himself to sleep, as Holly and Mark looked at each other with concern, confused about what just happened, and worried that it may happen again.

"Jesse, are you doing okay?" Mark asked to the back seat on the way home from school. Jesse sat quietly and continued to watch out the window. After looking through the rear-view mirror to check on his son, Mark continued on the road. Jesse hadn't said very much since the night terror, which worried both Mark and Holly. He was always the rambunctious, energetic kid; he became very withdrawn and scared, almost. Something happened that previous night, but what was it?

Jesse retreated to his room when they arrived at the house, neglecting to greet his future stepmother. With a butterfly bandage on her nose, Holly watched an empty little boy walk through the house almost as if he was a zombie. Concern and worry filled her face, looking to Mark only to see him shrugging his shoulders in defeat because he couldn't find out what was wrong. The household remained silent for a time, waiting for the right moment to bring up the night terror.

Dinner that night became awkwardly quiet: Jesse stared down at his food, maneuvering his green beans with his fork, and pushing his chicken around the plate; Mark and Holly looked at each other, almost as if silently fighting about who was going to talk first. Mark cleared his throat to speak but didn't have time to get a word out.

"Jesse," Holly spoke as she placed her hand on his wrist. "Please talk to us about last night, please." Jesse only looked at her with guilt in his eyes and didn't know what to say. "Jesse, you did nothing wrong, do you understand me?" she pleaded.

"I don't remember anything! I hurt you. I woke up and your nose was bleeding. I don't remember anything," he chanted over and over again, trying to comprehend those events.

"Jesse, calm down. It's called a night terror, okay? I was reading about them while you were in school. They happen a lot in kids like yourself, okay? It was a bad nightmare. You did nothing wrong." Holly got up from her chair, kneeled next to Jesse and placed both hands on his cheeks. "They say these can happen when you're under stress. Everything with Lizzie, the fights, moving to a new home. It's a lot to get used to all at once. It's going to be okay; do you hear me?" she asked as she wiped away tiny tears escaping his eyes and kissed his cheek. "It was an accident, my bloody nose. No one did it on purpose, it was an accident." She embraced Jesse in a tight hug and continued to tell him it was an accident and that it was going to be okay. A clearing throat was heard from across the table.

"Jesse, let me tell you something. I remembered this while I was working. I don't know how many people know this, and I don't know if I was supposed to say anything, but both of your sisters had night terrors when they were your age," Mark said softly. He was cautious to say anything more but watched as Holly let go of her embrace and looked at him with confusion. That fact was new to her; she returned to her seat, watching Mark with her head cocked to one side, anxious to hear what was going to be said next. Jesse paused where he was and hung on to every word his father said as he explained how Sophie and Lizzie had both gone through spurts of bad nightmares and night terrors when they were little kids growing up. A glimmer of hope filled Jesse's body as he learned that he wasn't weird or possessed or broken. He was a kid, and his sisters went through the same thing.

Days later, Jesse laid next to Lizzie in the

hospital bed as they watched cartoons on TV. Jesse fumbled with the tags on the blanket for a while, and the silence bothered Lizzie.

"What's going on, kid?" she asked.

"I had a bad dream, and I punched Holly in the nose. They said it was an accident, but I still feel sad," he explained. Lizzie hugged her little brother tightly, whispering that she used to have dreams like that too. Jesse leaned into her words, resting near her side.

"Do you want to know a secret?" Lizzie whispered. Jesse's eyes widened and crawled up to her face, eager to hear his sister's mystery.

"I used to have dreams… that would…. make me wet the bed," she admitted. Jesse laughed and giggled at the scandal, asking if there were any other weird things she did in her sleep. Lizzie confessed that Sophie would talk in her sleep, and that she would wake up in the middle of the night to their big sister doing ballet twirls in the middle of the bedroom, all while she was fast asleep. Jesse smiled humbly, feeling better that his sisters were weird sleepers too.

SOPHIE

Sophie played on her phone while sitting in the large green armchair that sat next to Lizzie's bed. Lizzie was fast asleep, recovering from physical therapy earlier that day. Mark walked down to the cafeteria to get him and Sophie something to eat. He was stuck in deep thought about his daughters' struggles as he wandered down the empty hallways, past conversing doctors and extra IV stands. He walked past the nurse's station, where a TV was playing on the news station. Updates about the hearings were being announced. They were well underway of presenting evidence against Superintendent Davidson, but the defense was also presenting a strong case on its side as well. Whispers and murmurs were heard from the nurses surrounding the station. Still frustrated about the whole ordeal of Leslie leaving, Mark shook his head and continued the long walk to the hospital cafeteria.

Lyla walked in with extra sheets for Lizzie's bed. She asked Sophie how she was doing, recognizing that Lizzie herself was fast asleep. Sophie and Lyla whispered for a few minutes about how the day was and how physical therapy went. It turned out Lizzie was only a couple weeks from being able to go home, and with how hard she worked in physical therapy, it was slated to even be earlier. Sophie walked up and gave Lyla a huge hug and thanked her for how well she was taking care of her little sister. After hearing a rustling in the bed on the other side of the room. They looked over to see a barely awake Lizzie staring back at them.

"Will it really only be a couple weeks?" she mumbled. She reached up and rubbed her eyes to try to wake up faster. Lyla nodded her head and smiled with excitement; she mentioned that she had to go check on her other patients, and that Sophie would fill her in on the rest. Mark walked back into the room shortly after Lyla left. Sophie told them both the news.

LIZZIE

Oh, my goodness, only a couple more weeks?! Ahhhhhhh! I couldn't believe it! The last few months had felt like years, but I could finally get out of that damn hospital room. I was going to live life again. Dad and Holly told me about their move into their new house, and that it had plenty of room for Jesse and me. I can finish school. I can breathe fresh air and not feel so trapped. The doctor said my progress in physical therapy was going to determine exactly when I get to go home. I was determined to be able to do it. I may not be able to walk anymore, but I wanted to be able to take care of myself again, and so I fought through the pain from my skin scarring over itself. That had been so difficult. My skin healed so tightly that my range of motion was not there yet. I couldn't lift my arm over my head, and when I was sitting up, it stretched the skin on my back far enough that it felt like it was going to tear.

It had been a couple weeks since I asked or even needed pain medication to cope through physical therapy. It hurt to feel like I needed medication to get by, to feel better. I didn't want it, but it was getting to the point again where the pain wouldn't stop. Lyla asked me if I would talk to one of her friends. I guess he was a therapist that helped people with chronic pain or something like that. I didn't know that would be something that had helped as much as it had. My days seemed a little brighter now, and the pain from physical therapy and daily life didn't feel so overwhelming.

I spent so much time in my own head since I had been there. Being stuck in a hospital bed for months didn't give me a whole lot else to do. And being someone who was used to taking care of herself, needing help with everything: rolling over, using the bathroom, etc. really messed with my head sometimes. To say I was excited to get out of there was a vast understatement.

Dad came into the room with food for him and Sophie. I was starving. I practically begged Sophie for the tub of chocolate pudding he brought for her. Luckily, being the best big sister, I was then the owner of a new tub of chocolate pudding. Dad went on about how he and Holly were planning everything to get me home and how excited Jesse was to have his big sister around again. They planned for Holly to pick up Jesse from school and bring him up to see me. They had been trying to see me around the weekends, but with them just moving, it had been a few weeks since Jesse had been able to come up. I was just excited to see him. Before the accident, we were inseparable; but then it became months before he came up to see me, so I relished every moment I could while he was there.

We sat around and talked about anything and everything for a while, waiting for Holly and Jesse to arrive. Sophie talked about how her kids were doing well in school and how Chris was working towards a potential promotion that would let them move closer. Dad talked about their move and showed us pictures of the new house that Holly had taken a few days before. The house looked beautiful: wrap-around porch, vaulted ceilings and a beautiful great room that had plenty of space for my wheelchair. He bragged about how he found the only things he was looking for in the new house: space for his kids to grow, and the ability to accommodate me. That made my heart melt. A few months ago, I hardly heard from Dad. He was always so absorbed in work, and he lived so far away, that he really wasn't involved in my life. It was just Mom. I could see how much he had changed over the last few months, and thankfully for the better.

I could vaguely hear childlike footsteps running down the hallway towards the door. Looking in that direction, I saw Jesse's shadow racing towards us, followed by Holly gliding in the background. He greeted me with the same excited glee that I was used to from that ball of energy, and I was healed enough that he was able to climb onto the bed with me. Dad met Holly at the door with a one-armed hug and a kiss to the forehead, and he began explaining how physical therapy had gone that day. He excused himself to get a little work done in the corner of the room, and Holly sat and talked with us kids. Most of the conversation consisted of answering all our questions about the wedding that was happening in the next few months. Sophie and I basked in all the wedding details. We were all so excited about that day and couldn't have been happier that it was with Holly. We conversed for almost an hour before Doctor James came in and gave updates on my progress. Sophie walked out of the room to call her husband and check on the kids.

I had to be able to wheel myself in my wheelchair before I was able to go home. I was so close, but my hands always felt completely raw after physical therapy. That was discouraging to hear. I felt there was no way I was going to be ready after two weeks. I withdrew into myself and got quiet. There was nothing else to say. I was preparing my mind for another few weeks in the hospital. Holly saw the disheartened look on my face and grabbed my hand.

"We will get through this, Lizzie. I promise. You'll be home soon."

"It's been more than 6 months, Holly. They know my hands are still not able to handle a lot of stress. Everything feels tight, like I can barely move. How will I ever get to the point where I can go home? Every time I get better, it's like I take 3 steps back. It's so frustrating," I muscled out between angry tears. She grabbed a tissue from the table to the side of the bed and dabbed away some of the loose tears, and she kept re-assuring me that everything will turn out for the better. She held my hand while I vented about being stuck in that hospital for months, feeling like I was never going to be able to leave. I just didn't care anymore. Any progress I made was somehow reset by more progress I needed to make, and I felt like it just wasn't worth it to try anymore. Holly sat and listened. She listened quietly to everything I said, and she kept squeezing my hand to somehow say she was still listening.

It felt like hours but was probably only a few minutes later when I ran out of things to say. I laid in that dreadful hospital bed crunched up into a ball trying to comfort myself. Holly sat in the armchair, her hands on her chin, thinking about what we could do. After more awkward silence, she mentioned that she saw a commercial not long ago about new gloves that were coming out, and maybe that would help me in physical therapy, and that it couldn't hurt to try. I nodded, still not feeling like talking, and she hopped on her phone and bought some online within a couple minutes. Dad walked in shortly after and noticed my somber demeanor. He asked if everything was okay, and Holly explained what the doctor had mentioned and how it was discouraging for me to meet a goal that felt seemingly impossible. He nodded his head in understanding and walked over to the bed to pat Jesse on the head.

After ushering Jesse over to his fiancé, Dad sat on the stool next to my bed and talked about some story he used to hear from Grandma Faulkner when she lived with us. It was a story about when Grandpa was drafted to fight in the war and had to leave Grandma with 6 kids to care for with measly resources. I guess the house they were living in started to fall apart, there was no heat, and food became more and more scarce. He explained that everything seemed to fall apart for Grandma, and she was just as angry at the world as I was. He asked me to remember my favorite thing about Grandma. After thinking for a while, I mentioned that we could ask her anything, and she'd have some fortune cookie-like wisdom that couldn't come from anywhere else.

"That wisdom didn't come from anywhere, Lizzie," Dad started. "GG needed to go through a lot to be able to know what to say. She's an incredibly strong and smart woman, and I think it's safe to say we all look up to her, even me. I see a lot of her in you, young lady. The struggles you have gone through have given you wisdom I could only dream of having. You have taken the paralysis and skin treatments like an actual Viking. I've seen and heard some of the conversations you have had with Jesse. You are a Faulkner, Lizzie. You can do this. We will help you get through this, no matter how long it takes or what we must do, okay?" he said almost sternly. He took my hand in one hand and patted my head with his other. "Kick their ass, kiddo." I heard Jesse in the background whisper "YES!" and I couldn't help but smile.

FRESH

LESLIE

The hearing was not going well. It was obvious that Superintendent Davidson had connections on the board, but there wasn't a way to call out those individuals and ask them to step down. Matt's job became harder and harder with each passing day to try changing the minds of the individuals sitting in front of him. Every case of mistreatment of staff and students got overshadowed by Davidson's lawyers filibustering about every budget crisis he averted and various education reforms he instituted in the school district. They brought up his cooperation of state standards with their new standards and reforms. Mention of neglect of building codes and safety violations prompted them to bring up the amount of fundraising he delivered to the school in his control.

There seemed to be no way they would win

this case. Matt told Leslie and Emily that they needed their smoking gun, their secret weapon. They sat at the dining room table in the condo Leslie was staying in, drinking tea and flipping through all the paperwork they had collected, all the cases they produced, and sending mass texts to the parent group trying to find that one piece of evidence they needed to corner Davidson. At this point, they were getting desperate.

"I know Lizzie probably can't leave the hospital right now," Matt started, "But what if we recorded her telling her story and what her journey looks like? That would be a powerful, emotional pull."

"But we have all these numbers. Why can't you work with that?" Leslie mentioned with a scathing tone.

"Leslie, I am doing the best I can. There's only so far I can go with this. And you saw Davidson's legal team. Without a pull, we don't have a chance."

"I'm not using my daughter as a circus act."

"It's not a circus act, Leslie. It's our chance," Matt pleaded.

"No," Leslie commanded. Matt gave up on

the plan, and they kept brainstorming. After breaking out the wine and drinking for what seemed like hours, Emily had fallen asleep on the couch, leaving Matt and Leslie to strategize alone. The floor lamp in the corner of the room produced just enough light for them to see each other. Neither of them realized the sun had gone down. Leslie finished off her glass and picked up the bottle to feel that it too was empty. Matt shrugged his shoulders and mentioned that there was no wine left in the house. He stood to throw away the empty bottles and place the glasses in the sink, while Leslie placed her head in her hands and tried to think through their next steps.

"I don't know what to do now. Nothing is working. It wasn't supposed to be this hard," she vented to Matt, who was rinsing the glasses and washing his hands. She continued to vent about how this was supposed to be over months ago, and Davidson couldn't have possibly had this much power on the board. Matt suggested the emotional pull of Lizzie's story, but Leslie wouldn't listen. She angrily pushed the scattered piles of paper and notebooks away from her sight, some falling off the table and onto the floor. Matt made haste to get to Leslie's side before she destroyed the place again. He grabbed her wrists and told her to calm down, and that he wouldn't bring it up again. He reminded her that she had a lot to drink and wouldn't do that normally. Leslie tried to break from his grasp, but Matt held her in a bear hug and wouldn't let go until she calmed down. He sat her back down in the chair and knelt to pick the files up off the floor.

"We need to take a break. It's clear we aren't getting anywhere right now. We are all exhausted and have been doing this for hours," he stated while pointing at Emily. Leslie rolled her eyes and started mumbling something under her breath, something that Matt couldn't understand. He shrugged it off, assuming it was another one of her drunk aphorisms and continued to clean up the paperwork spread across the table. He cleared his throat and suggested that Leslie go to bed and get some rest. Leslie raised her fist, flipping him off and then folding her arms, pouting at the obscene request. He wasn't going to tell her what to do.

Leslie got up from her chair and walked past Matt on her way to her room, elbowing his side on the way. Matt doubled over in pain and grabbed her arm. After sternly telling her she was not to do that again, he let her go in order to finish cleaning the kitchen and checking on Emily. The rest of the evening remained quiet and isolated, each person involved with their own beings.

LIZZIE

I woke up from an early afternoon nap to see a man in a suit that I didn't recognize. I looked over to see Dad standing between him and me, his hand on his chin looking like he was trying to decide what to think of this guy. I cleared my throat, getting their attention, and the man introduced himself as Matt, the lawyer that was helping Mom with the hearings. Dad asked what he was doing there, to which Matt explained that Mom didn't know he was there.

"I need your help, Lizzie. I was hoping to be able to use your story to help our case. I know we can't get you out of the hospital at the moment, but if I could record your story, your time here in the hospital, things like that, but that would really help us," he explained. I looked bewildered towards my dad, who was then sitting in the armchair next to my bed, still thinking. He looked like he didn't trust Matt. Granted, I didn't know if I did either.

"Something about this feels off. Do you really think you need to use my daughter in this way for your case?" Dad asked. Matt explained that the case didn't look great, and if they wanted to make a dent, they needed a smoking gun. Dad looked at me and asked what I thought. I really didn't have an opinion either way. However, the longer I thought about it, the more I wanted to do something to help. Sophie and I went to school there, and I had been helping with STEM there for a couple years. It was almost like home to me. I looked to Dad, who was waiting for my answer. He reassured me that it was my decision.

"If there is anything I can do to help the school, and the teachers teaching there, I will do it," I answered. Dad sighed as Matt perked up. He asked if there was anything I needed or anything I needed to do before I felt comfortable enough to be on camera. I requested Holly be there to help me, to which Dad jumped to his phone and called her. As soon as she could that afternoon, she and Jesse walked into the hospital room prepared and ready to help in every way they could. Holly tried to tie my hair back and adjust the baby blue hospital gown, making sure I was covered where I was comfortable. Jesse sat on Dad's lap, mesmerized at the commotion in the room. Matt pulled out his phone and turned on his camera. He didn't have any questions or requests, other than, "Please tell your story."

After a few minutes of recording, Matt expressed his gratitude, shook Dad's hand and left. Dad asked me that I had thought about the situation, and if I was happy with what I shared.

"I'm glad I was able to help somehow. I just

want to find ways to help so I don't feel like such a burden."

"You're not a burden," he reassured me. He kissed the top of my head and announced he was going to go grab some takeout for the rest of the family. Holly, Jesse, and I played are round of cards before he got back.

LESLIE

It seemed like day 365 of hearings and presentations of evidence for Leslie. No matter what they brought to the table, it seemed like Davidson's defense had a cause or alibi. It didn't make sense. Luckily, they were nearing the end, and as the meetings ended late that afternoon, Matt asked for one more piece of the story to be added to the case. Davidson's defense gave the okay, since they were confident they hit a home run. A large projector screen lowered itself from the ceiling on the side of the room. Matt plugged in his laptop to connect and press play. Bewilderment struck Leslie's face as she came face to face to her daughter talking about her story.

"I wanted to do this to help the school, the kids, and the teachers. I don't remember a lot of what happened, nor do I really remember a lot of what happened earlier that day either. I was in a coma for about a month. When I woke, that's when the doctor told me about the burns. It was a while later when I realized I couldn't feel my legs. I'm 17 years old. I will no longer walk again. I used to do everything myself, but now I need help with even the smallest of tasks. I was slated to graduate early, and that dream has also been lost. I can't run with my brother, or with my nieces and nephew and play. I have been in this hospital for months recovering from burns and continuous skin grafts. Physical therapy is still excruciating. Some days, I feel like so much of a burden that I don't want to exist." Leslie looked about the room to see no one with a dry eye. "If the building was up to code, this may not have happened. If not me, who would it have been? I hope you make the right decision." The board excused for a short recess, after which the sides would present their closing arguments. Leslie rushed out of the room as fast as she could, with Matt chasing closely behind. He kept yelling for her to slow down, but she kept walking faster. Her face had adopted a shade of red so pigmented, it showed through her TV makeup. Matt finally caught up to her and grabbed her arm.

"I had to do it," Matt pleaded.

"You did NOT," Leslie replied sternly. "You said we could do this with the numbers, with the stories, with the proof. Why did you go behind my back and force my daughter to relive that? Why did you not tell me?”

“I knew you wouldn’t approve. She wanted to do it. Mark was there; he let her have the decision. We needed a smoking gun. I TOLD you that. Many times. We weren’t going to win without it,” Matt tried to explain.

“And if we don’t win, you used my daughter for the attention you wanted, and we gained nothing,” Leslie barked.

“You’re lecturing me about doing things for attention?” Matt asked. Leslie bit her tongue and stared at him with an eye-piercing glare. She slapped him in the face so hard, it took no time for a subtle pink mark to appear on Matt’s right side of his face. They remained as far away from each other as they possibly could until the session reconvened.

SOPHIE

Jesse ran down the long hospital hallway to meet Lizzie and Sophie, who had just come out of the rehabilitation unit from physical therapy. Sophie had to jump in front of her sister to catch the rambunctious child from trying to jump into her lap. Mark and Holly trailed behind, watching their kids re-unite after a couple weeks of being away. They spun around the massive hallway, seeing how dizzy they could get. A health scare at the hospital prevented visitors from entering for a few days, and Jesse's school trip kept them away from the hospital for even longer. Upon meeting at the doors, Sophie updated the family on Lizzie's progress. There was supposed to be a meeting with her doctor before the shutdown, so they re-scheduled for that day. As everyone walked towards Lizzie's room, they passed by a large TV screen that sat above the nurse's station.

A young man with a nervous, freckled face reported from the state capital about updates with the hearings. Protesters still threw their signs in the air and chanted at the motionless building. After months of fighting, evidence revealing, and negotiations, it was decided that the case was to be dropped. Superintendent Davidson would retain his current position. The board approved additional funds to be used on repairing the school, but reparations for injuries related to the accident weren't priority. The fight was over. The reporter walked up the stone steps to find Emily, Matt, and Leslie grouped together mumbling about the results of the hearing.

"Leslie, what are your thoughts about the results of the hearings?" he asked, passing the microphone over to the group. Leslie froze where she was and wiped a rogue tear from her eye. Matt noticed the emotion and stepped forward, taking control of the mic and the conversation for the group. Emily put her arm around Leslie and hugged her as they both started to sob. Matt tried to hide his disappointment in the interview, but his face told a very different story. His furrowed brow and flushed cheeks let the camera know that this wasn't just a professional decision from the board. His stern tone and shaky voice told the interviewer that this was personal.

"We are going to find a way to continue to fight this. This individual does not deserve to work in a field with other people, let alone our children. This decision has the potential to cause more harm to the community, and I will not stop until the community is safe," he practically barked at the end of his speech, turning to usher Emily and Leslie down the steps and to the parking lot. The ladies covered their teary faces while they walked down the steps and across the street to the car, doing their best to avoid all the publicity that sparked from the hearing.

Jessie, Sophie, and Lizzie watched their mother on the television screen walk down the steps, heartbroken to see their mom so emotional. They joined in a group hug together, watching the somber events unfold before their eyes. Mark and Holly whispered to each other how confused they were that the hearings ended the way they did, but also how grateful they were that part of the journey was over. That drama was out of their lives, and they could take a step forward. And hopefully, just hopefully, Leslie would feel the same way, too.

LIZZIE

Man, I wish life wasn't so intense all the time. I was just about ready to get released from the hospital, and then I learned that the case with Superintendent Davidson was getting dismissed. It really didn't matter to me what the result was, but seeing my mom so devastated broke my heart. She was still my mom after all, even after everything that we'd been through the last few months. It just hurt seeing that. I asked Dad if he knew whether Mom was going to move back home, but I guess they hadn't talked in a while, so no one knew what was happening. At that point, I was just glad things were finally calming down and, he found someone that was going to make him happy.

The gloves that Holly ordered were helping in therapy a bit. I guess they were specially made for people who suffered bad burns on their hands to be able to work with them more easily. They gripped the wheelchair a lot easier than my exposed, bare hands could, so thank goodness I had them. I could only roll the wheelchair down the hallway and back, which the doctor said was about 300 feet, which was cool. I was not going to be spending my days wheeling around everywhere all day every day. I made enough progress that he said I could go home in a couple days. Holly and Jesse had been helping me pack up everything I'd acquired in my months and months of being in the hospital. Amongst the giant stash of socks, medical supplies, clothes, and decks of cards, they ended up finding a letter from Lyla tucked in between a couple of blankets she had given me weeks ago. Holly asked me if I wanted to read it, but I had just gotten back from physical therapy, and I was wiped. I asked her to read it to me so I could rest, but I didn't know what this letter was going to be. Holly opened the envelope, which also contained about $50 in cash folded into the letter:

Lizzie,

> *Over the past few months, I have absolutely loved getting to know you. Seeing you grow, heal, and process all the events of the accident has been so inspirational to see, especially knowing how young you are. You are absolutely wiser than your years, and I know you are on your way to accomplish incredible things in your*

future. You have more dedication and perseverance in your right hand than most of my co-workers do in their entire body (winky face). Your resilience is contagious. Spread it around. Please, don't forget this part of the journey. Share it with others and let them know that anything is possible if you believe that it is possible. I want you to fight for your dreams as hard as I've seen you fight for your life. I want to continue to see you flourish in school. I want to hear you on the news and social media changing the world with your unique view on life. Your love for others and positive outlook will continue to be an incredible example to your little brother and even your big sister, and I know that you are so much stronger than you believe yourself to be. Remember that. Remember that always. You have an extraordinary gift. Use it. You've taught me to fight for what I want, and I'm going to do that, for you. I absolutely love you, Lizzie, and will always be here for you even when you leave this room. I've inserted my phone number below (don't tell anyone, we're technically not supposed to do this), so please keep in touch and let me know if you need anything. Anything.

     I will for sure be there to see you get discharged.   *Love, Lyles*

SOPHIE

Holly walked out of the dressing room in a gown that shouted that she was a queen. Elegant stones hugged her sides, and her train draped so gracefully off her shoulders that she glowed. Sophie sat on the sofa in front of the wall of mirrors and had Lizzie on video chat so she could see too. All the girls teared up at the sight of the dress. Fifth dress of the day, and that was the one. The girls could hear Jesse asking what was wrong on the other end of the phone, running to Lizzie's bedside and trying to see what was on the camera. Lyla was quick to cover the phone, and Lizzie explained that they were happy tears, and the wedding was going to be amazing. Jesse pouted briefly from not being included, but easily got over it to continue playing monster trucks in the corner of the room. After having a long, emotional mother-daughter moment together, everyone wiped their tears and agreed that this was the dress Holly was to wear to the wedding. From the other end of the phone, Lizzie heard Holly mention that the bridesmaids' dresses were already made and ready to go, and they would all see them when they got home.

A few hours later, Mark walked into the hospital room with Holly, Sophie and Chris for the special day. Mark announced that everything at home was ready, and that he hoped Lizzie would like where they lived, only to be cut off by Jesse affirming the idea and babbling about how much he loved the house. Sophie gave Lizzie flowers to congratulate her; large pink roses to match the rose gold décor they had used for her bedroom. Lyla barged into the room and declared to the crowd that she had Grandma Faulkner on her phone video chatting so she could be a part of this special day.

"Dad, have you heard anything from Mom?" Lizzie asked. "She wanted this more than me some days. I would have thought she would be here for this." Mark shrugged his shoulders and shook his head with defeat. They had been trying to contact Leslie for days, but to no avail. She picked up the phone once, only to hang it up as quickly as she answered when she heard Mark's voice. Mark explained that they would still try to contact her and let her visit the house because she still is their mother, but not to let her absence taint the excitement of that day. Doctor James came in and pulled Mark and Holly aside to talk about the paperwork that needed signed and aftercare that was needed. Jesse, Sophie, and Lizzie played a few rounds of paper, rock, scissors together while Chris sat in an empty chair next to the window and checked his phone.

LYLA

Lyla cleaned up cords and equipment while they were waiting. She smiled at the sight of these three siblings laughing and playing around, 3 young people who went through so much in their lives in the past few months, but that day were sitting around each other smiling and laughing and just being together. Her heart melted at the sight of this family that she watched come together so closely to support each other, and this young girl she cared for since the day the accident happened. She was heartbroken that she wouldn't see this little girl every day, but she knew this was her job. She helped someone heal.

Her favorite part of the job was seeing her patients get better, but this one was different. Lizzie changed her. She watched this teenage girl come in with third degree burns all over her body and find out she can no longer walk, but this young girl's strength astonished Lyla. Even though Lizzie went through incredible struggles both physically and psychologically, she somehow came out of this alive and persevered through some of the most inconceivable pain she had ever witnessed a patient experience. It wasn't something Lyla would ever wish upon a worst enemy, but here this young girl was, smiling and content. Where this girl came from, Lyla would never know, but one thing was for sure. Life was not going to be the same.

She could picture a future telling all the new nurses about a girl who came in, a girl who wasn't ever supposed to come out. She envisioned checking social media in the future to see this young girl graduating from medical school, or even becoming president. She imagined running into this young girl at the store and seeing how much she had grown and sprouted. She hoped Lizzie would never forget her and would only remember the good times in this miserable hospital. She crossed her fingers that Lizzie would never forget her impeccable poker skills, and that she would hit it big somewhere. She was going to miss this girl.

This day was the exciting, terrifying, nerve-wracking and beautiful day which was Lizzie being released. She couldn't bring herself to tell them she was leaving the hospital for a NICU job in another nearby hospital. Not yet. This wasn't her day. It was Lizzie's. She needed to be there to see her released. Then she would let them in on the news. She wondered if Lizzie got the letter she left.

TWINKLE

FAMILY

Mark, Holly, and Doctor James walked back into the room to announce paperwork was completed, and Lizzie was officially being discharged. Lyla pulled Lizzie's wheelchair into the room, and Mark positioned himself at the side of the bed to lift his daughter into the chair. With one arm under her back and the other below her thighs, he carried her scarred body with ease. Lizzie smiled while she was set into the chair, knowing this no longer subjected her to the immense, burning pain that it once did. As a family, everyone walked down the gloomy hospital hallway for the last time. Lyla met them all at the front door, hugged Lizzie and let her know how proud she was, and how powerful Lizzie would be.

"Thank you, Lyla, for being such an amazing friend, and for being here every step of the way," Lizzie replied. "I couldn't have gotten here without you, and you'll always hold a special place in my heart. Thank you." Tears filled both their eyes as the reality hit that their lives would be different now, daily visits and poker games wouldn't be the normal anymore. The family embraced Lyla together in gratitude for everything she had done, and everyone wished each other the best. Mark gave Doctor James one last handshake, and the family walked out of the automatic doors for the last time.

Lizzie rolled into the three-bedroom farmhouse, Mark, Holly, and Jesse following behind. It was completely different, and she felt uncomfortable at first being in such a new place. Jesse ran around the wheelchair, offering to show Lizzie around the new house and brag about his new Batman themed bedroom, right after he showed her his recently acquired collection of foam dart guns. Mark and Holly dropped all the bags in the entryway for the time being, waiting for the moment to calm down and for Lizzie to feel more at home before unloading all her belongings.

Lizzie started to sob a little bit as she toured the rest of the house. It felt so different to her, almost like she was the imposter showing up to a house that was not hers. She had lived in her mother's home her entire life. She knew nothing different other than recent months in the hospital. Holly hugged her and wiped away her rogue tears; she kept re-assuring Lizzie that it was going to be okay. She mentioned that it was okay to feel uncomfortable for the moment. Holly reminded her she was so used to the hospital and her mother's previous home that there was a chance she would feel this way no matter where she went, but that the family was there for her. Lizzie nodded her head and smiled softly in understanding. Jesse hopped up and sat in Lizzie's lap, embracing her in a warm hug, and he held on.

Mark suggested that they all gather in the living room and watch a movie to calm down from the exciting, busy day. He pushed the wheelchair over to the side of the suede sofa and patted Lizzie on the head while Holly grabbed a movie to watch. Lizzie grabbed a tissue from the nearby oak side table and patted away her face, Jesse still clutching around her shoulders. Halfway through the movie, Mark looked over to see both his children fast asleep in the chair. After nudging Holly to look at the innocent, wholesome scene, he got up from the couch and wheeled the kids down the hallway to their bedrooms. Even while fast asleep, Jesse didn't let go of his grasp from Lizzie. With the help of Holly, Mark lifted both children from the wheelchair into Lizzie's queen size bed.

"It finally feels like our family is complete," Holly whispered as they stood in the doorway watching their children sleep. The rest of the night remained quiet. It was the first night of peace in months. Maybe now, the family could move forward into a final, new normal. The next few days found themselves full of emotions, full of busy. Jesse started school again, and Lizzie found it more difficult to adjust than she imagined. Random, silent bouts throughout the day found themselves being filled with Lizzie's silent tears. Her wheelchair found itself hitting all the furniture all the time, and the aching in her hands made itself known as she pulled up to the table for dinner. Holly found herself in Lizzie's room every night encouraging her that things would get better.

FAMILY

"It sucks that everything takes so much time. But now, it takes even more time because I'm broken," Lizzie would often say. Holly sat endless night hours in Lizzie's bed cradling her teenager to sleep, continually telling her that she wasn't broken. She wasn't broken. As the wedding got closer, Lizzie started to find more joy in the fairy tale she was soon to be a part of. She forgot about feeling broken. Holly brought her to every appointment for the wedding planning, and Lizzie's eyes twinkled seeing all the wedding preparations taking place: the raspberry marbled three-tier cake, the sparkling chandeliers chosen to hang from the ceilings, the jewelry that would grace Holly's neck. Lizzie's mind forgot about recovery; she started to dream about her own fairy tale.

Sophie placed the brown sandals on Lizzie's feet while Holly adjusted the flowers sitting in her hair. Jesse ran around in his new button-down shirt and yellow bow tie. The plan to get him into the matching suspenders was put on hold while the rest of the family got ready for the ceremony. Family and friends gathered inside the venue, greeting one another with smiles and hugs aplenty. Couples danced around the enormous ballroom floor to the background music playing, and others sat around the bar enjoying a drink. Friends re-acquainted themselves; family got to know each other again. Jesse kept running through all the groups of people present, yelling "Surprise!" at every flabbergasted face he saw. Even with all the joy in the grand open space, there was still an elephant in the room for the family. The guests didn't know what this family learned days earlier.

Mark, Holly, and all the children were enjoying a pre-wedding dinner together. As everyone was sitting around the table enjoying their steaming chicken dinner, Holly announced that a letter came in the mail. She ripped open the envelope and skimmed the contents of the letter. She looked to Mark, her eyebrows raised, and forehead wrinkled, but Mark encouraged her to read it anyways. The contents knocked the wind out of everyone in the family:

> *Kids,*
>
> *I hope you all are doing well, and that your father is taking care of you... or at least trying. I'm staying here at the capital. I kinda like it here. You know I want you here, but that's obviously not going to happen since apparently living with your father is sooooo much better than living with your mother. You could have told me that instead of stringing me on saying that you wanted me to visit. Lizzie, glad the doctors finally got their shit together and got you out of that place. They only kept you there so they could screw us financially. Oh well. Good luck to us paying your bills. You better get to walking so we can figure this out. Sophie, it's a good thing you've been at your sister's side, but you need to focus on your own kids.*

They need you more. Chris can't do it himself. You need to be home. Jesse, little Jesse, I hope the fights at school stopped. You know I'm not coming down anymore, right? Just keep that in mind next time some big kid calls you a wuss. Win the fight or step down.

Mark, if you do anything to those kids, I swear to God, I'll sue you like I sued the state, and I know I will win next time. You and that harlot can do what you want, but do not smear my name in front of my kids. They already need therapy, don't give them more reasons to need it. Good luck on that fancy wedding of yours. Just another way to turn my kids against me.

I might write later. I might not. No idea. Going out on the town with some lawyers from the hearings, sooooo... have fun.

Leslie

Tears streamed down Holly's face while she read the letter to the family. The room was eerily silent, the only sound being the tick-tock from the clock hanging on the wall nearby. Mark's face went beet red, and the fork he was using to pick up the baked chicken and vegetables bent under the pressure of his grasp. Jesse looked at Holly confused, while Lizzie and Sophie's mouths dropped to the ground. Chris's eyebrows furled, softening only to his oldest child asking what the letter meant. He sat the child on his lap and cleared his throat, thinking about what he wanted to say. Suddenly, Mark grabbed the letter from Holly's hands and crumpled the paper, throwing it across the room.

"That is not your mother. I don't know who or what that was, but that was not the mother you or I knew. Do not listen to those words. Do not take any of that to heart or believe any of it! Do you hear me? She is the one that left. She is the one that abandoned all of you and decided her dreams were more important than supporting her children. If that means I'm smearing her name, so be it. I will not sit here and listen to a cowardly, selfish being belittle the same life she created. That is not fair to any of you." Holly tried to usher Mark to sit down and be quiet, but he continued to rant about how this was not the way he wanted his children and grandchildren to be treated, and how cruel it was to not answer anyone's calls, and to write a demeaning letter to essentially say goodbye. "How disconnected is she? Jesse hasn't had a fight in months. Sophie is an incredible sister, and an extraordinary mother to her kids. The fact she thinks Sophie needs to 'stay home' is not right. And she knows that Lizzie is paralyzed. Telling her that the only way to pay bills is to get her walking is unwarranted. I will not stand for this!" he yelled, slamming his fists on the table, which made everyone at the table jump.

All the faces in the room had tears in their eyes. Sophie had ushered the smaller kids into Jesse's room to play because they had gotten so scared. She sat outside the bedroom door on her knees bawling in her arms, while Chris kneeled next to her and had his arm around her shoulders. Lizzie's face became almost purple from trying to keep on a brave face. Holly wiped the tears from Lizzie's face and kept whispering that it was going to be okay, and not to worry. After what seemed like a lifetime of Mark ranting and screaming to himself in the kitchen, he sat down in the chair and laid his head in his hands for the time being. After a few moments of silence, he looked up at his emotional children.

"Shit, I'm sorry. This wasn't a conversation that was yours to hear," he admitted as he watched his daughters. "That letter…… that letter…. I spent a long time away from you guys. When Leslie and I split, I stepped away. I wasn't the father that I needed to be, but this is me now. You kids are my life, now.

I want you guys to understand that. I can see that what your mother said hurt you. It hurt all of us. I don't know what someone could be feeling to write something like that to their own children. I do want you all to have a relationship with your mom, but I'm leaving it completely up to you. Remember, I will always be here to protect you, okay?" He stopped speaking for a moment to see Lizzie and Sophie's responses. After wiping away more tears, they nodded their heads, and Mark continued to re-assure them that things were going to be okay and kept apologizing for the anger he showed in that moment. After he looked to Holly and apologized again for going off, he asked humbly if she was still willing to marry him.

"Mark, if I didn't want to marry you, I wouldn't have stayed all these months."

FAMILY

Twinkle lights hung from the ceiling beams, illuminating the ballroom with sparkling, flickering rays. Daffodils and Calla Lilies sat in mini vases on the square tables spread amongst the room surrounded by the subtle glow of various sizes of tea light candles. As everyone took their seats, soft voices sang in the background to the music coming over the speaker system. The officiant made his way down the aisle and took his place under the vine covered archway, announcing the event was about to begin. The family lined the hallway next to the room, preparing to walk down the aisle. Sophie, Lizzie, and Holly embraced each other in one last group hug before lining the hallway.

Music started to play, and Mark walked down the aisle in his navy-blue velvet suit, Jesse right at his side. Chris followed behind with his children, who played the role of flower girls and ring bearer. The rest of the bridal party followed, including Sophie and Lizzie in their sunflower yellow bridesmaids' dresses. The music slowly changed, announcing Holly's appearance. She walked down the aisle in her pearly white, mermaid gown, glowing under the twinkle lights and candlelit tables. The highlight on her cheeks glistened like the stars, and her smile glowed through her bright red lipstick. In the wake of Leslie's seemingly dramatic exit, the wedding was near perfect. All eyes were on Mark and Holly as they recited their vows, joking about Mark's obscenely loud chewing noises and Holly's penguin waddle when in heels that were too high.

"Sophie, Lizzie, and Jesse. Will you step forward?" the officiant asked over the microphone. The kids stepped forward out of the line and looked to the center of the room. "Your father wanted you to be a part of this beautiful ceremony. When I spoke with him, he mentioned how grateful he was that he was prompted to come back into your lives and have the second chance he needed to be a father to you and be involved in your lives. Holly says you are her children, no matter where you came from. One question I have for you three, is do you approve of this union between your father and Holly?" All the kids nodded in excitement, Sophie and Lizzie wiping away happy sobs. Holly reached around and held hands with Sophie and Lizzie; Mark turned and hugged his son. The ceremony continued, until the officiant announced:

"I now pronounce you husband, wife, and family. You may now kiss your bride." Mark and Holly embraced in a loving kiss, only before quickly turning and holding their children in a warm, family hug. Claps and cheers filled the room while the family held on to each other in utter joy. Amid the bodies, Jesse perked up in the center.

"We are a family."

Burn Unit

Burn Unit

ACKNOWLEDGMENTS

Thank you, Pat, for all your help editing and all your excitement for this project.

Thank you, Ashley, for showing us small-town girls that we can do something different, and it just might work. Thank you for paving the way, for all your advice and input, and for the amazing cover.

ABOUT THE AUTHOR

T. Michelle was born in a small, rural Idaho town, where she spent most of her life around the hustling, bustling ranching life that her family shared. Throughout various struggles in her adolescence and early adulthood, T. used writing to evoke the emotion she never knew how to convey otherwise. What started as a task planned only to say, "I did it to say I did it," Burn Unit is the first of hopefully many other writing projects planned for T. as she reminds herself why she loved writing so much.

www.ingramcontent.com/pod-product-compliance
Lightning Source LLC
Chambersburg PA
CBHW010741310726
48971CB00010B/2905